# ANNIKA
# ALONE

SHARON GRAHAM

# ANNIKA ALONE

iUniverse books may be ordered through booksellers or by contacting:

iUniverse
1663 Liberty Drive
Bloomington, IN 47403
www.iuniverse.com
844-349-9409

ISBN: 978-1-6632-2992-2 (sc)
ISBN: 978-1-6632-2993-9 (e)

Library of Congress Control Number: 2022902259

Print information available on the last page.

iUniverse rev. date: 02/24/2022

*With gratitude and love, this book is presented*
*in memory of Rex and Lillie Wilkinson,*
*my parents, and Ron Graham, my husband.*

# CONTENTS

# ACKNOWLEDGMENTS

My heartfelt appreciation and thanks go to Carol Krews, Brenda Davis, and Candy Holloway, who read drafts, offered support and encouragement, and provided a nudge when necessary. Thank you for being you.

I'm also indebted to novelist Louise Marley and Long Ridge Writers Group for nurturing my desire to write.

My gratitude also goes to iUniverse representatives, who consistently provided professional, focused, and productive expertise to accomplish the task at hand.

# AUTHOR'S NOTE

The historical content of this book is supported by extensive reading and research. The rivers, lakes, and timberland of the St. Croix River Valley provide a majestic setting for the story. An authentic flavor of mid-nineteenth-century Minnesota frontier life permeates the organizations listed below, and their contributions to this endeavor are appreciated.

- Gammelgarden Museum, 20880 Olinda Trail, Scandia, MN
- Minnesota Historical Sites, Oliver H. Kelly Farm, 15788 Kelly Farm Road, Elk River, MN 55330
- Stone House Museum, 241 Fifth Street, Marine of St. Croix, MN 55047
- Taylors Falls Queen Scenic Excursions, Taylor Falls, MN 55084
- Washington County Historical Society, PO Box 167, Stillwater, MN 55082

## CHAPTER 1

# THE INCIDENT

Annika opened Mamma's Bible and turned to the family record pages, which were neatly filled in with birth and death dates. She carefully inked in Mamma's date of death—May 15, 1865— and blew on the page to dry it. *Fourteen years old is too young to be left all alone in the world.* She returned the Bible to the writing table drawer.

Annika and her mother had shared the servants' quarters for nearly two years. Now, as the Browns' maid, she occupied this small room sparsely filled with quality furnishings. The room seemed large and empty. It was painful to spend time alone in the room. That evening, while the Browns were away, she was using her free time to confront her losses. She was on her own now, and she had to face the facts. Her eyes brimmed with tears as she took the jewelry box hand-carved by Pappa from the top of the four-drawer oak bureau, where it had sat untouched since Mamma's death.

She returned to her chair and rested the box on her lap. She opened it, and a faint fragrance of lavender tickled her nose. She removed a small bound book—Mamma's diary. The pages were written in Swedish script with only a few English words, but Annika was able to read an entry.

May 1856

We set sail today. The ocean is everywhere, and the weather is clear and mild. Annika is seasick. Isak loves this adventure.

Warm memories of Mamma comforted Annika as she read. She would read the entire diary, and then she would continue her family's dream by writing her own story.

She looked through the packet of letters tied with a blue ribbon and recognized Mormor Svensson's handwriting. Most of the return addresses were from Sweden. One envelope, postmarked a month before Mamma's death, was from Minnesota. It was written in English. She read.

Washington County, Minnesota
April 18, 1865

Dear Emelie,
Kjerstin and I are sad to know of the hard times you have endured. We pray you and Annika are well and safe. We welcome you to our home, if you wish to come. We are family. I will come east in the fall on business. Would you and Annika be able to return with me then? I will wait for your answer.

Your cousin,
Noak

The letter confused Annika. Mamma had never mentioned leaving New York. She needed to write to them about Mamma's death, but the thought of going to Minnesota frightened her.

She laid the letter aside and returned to the jewelry box. Three tiny folded squares of paper identified by dates attracted her attention. She opened one with her birth date—October 10,

1851—and discovered a lock of satin white hair. A tiny smile curled her lips when she realized her hair color had not changed. The other two squares of paper contained locks of Isak's and Rebecka's hair.

Annika laid aside the contents of the box and slipped her fingernail into a crevice along the bottom of it, and a thin sheaf of wood lifted. Stashed beneath the false bottom Annika found money. She counted out $12.18. Mamma had been saving for the move. Annika replaced everything except Noak's letter and returned the jewelry box to its place on the bureau.

Annika wondered, *Is working for the Browns and visiting the cemetery regularly all I want from life?* Some days, just getting through the day was a difficult challenge. What did she want? Had she given up on her family's dream of security in America?

Annika found her mother's tablet and pencil. She had to respond to Noak's letter.

New York City
January 24, 1866

Dear Noak,
Today I found your letter to Mamma. I am sorry to write so late. Mamma died in May from consumption. Please write to tell our family in Sweden about Mamma. I am alone and sad. Just now I am starting to go on with life. It is hard. I do not know about coming to Minnesota. Mamma did not tell me about her plan. I am glad to be in touch with family. Please come see me when you come east again.

Your cousin,
Annika

Weeks later, in the dark of night, Annika stirred in bed. Was that a muffled thud in the hallway, or was it her imagination? Her ears harkened to silence. She pulled at her pillow and nestled back into the warmth of her coverlet. A creak of a floorboard and a door opening and closing stole her breath. *It's nothing. Nothing,* she lied to herself. But the looming dark figure over her bed and the draft on her exposed legs left no doubt. Her throat was dry. Goose bumps covered her body. This was drastically wrong. She tried to sit up, but a hairy, weathered arm crushed against her chest and pinned her to the bed. A rough hand clamped over her mouth stifled her scream. *No!*

"Be quiet, and you won't get hurt." Brown's hot, foul breath scorched her face like a furnace. The pungent odor of pipe tobacco choked her. Terror seized her. He was on top of her like some crazed animal. All she could do was endure the unspeakable. She shut her eyes and willed her mind to take her anyplace but there.

The pressure and rage lasted an eternity. Sharp stubble scratched across her cheek. She tried to pull away, but he was determined to whisper in her ear.

"If you tell anyone of this, you will regret it," he hissed.

Finally, the weight lifted, and the bedroom door closed behind him. Silence coaxed Annika to open her eyes. Moonlight from the window gave the room an eerie aura, and Annika knew her life was forever altered. Every inch of her body ached as if hundreds of horses' hooves had pounded her into the dirt.

She stumbled from bed, scrambled to grasp the key waiting in the lock, and turned it. "I know I locked that," she muttered. Her trembling body slumped against the door, and she dwindled to the floor and sat with her back against the closed door, afraid to move. Never again could she feel safe within those walls. Annika sobbed. She slept when there were no more tears.

She awoke emotionally spent. Bathing and dressing exhausted her and brought no relief. She wadded her night clothing and bedding into a tight bundle, took them to the trash barrel behind the storage shed, stuffed them into the barrel, and lit a match. Who cared what Mrs. Brown thought? Likely, the woman wouldn't even notice a missing sheet or two. If only the flames could have reduced the sickening memory to ashes. Anger and grief sealed her in a cocoon of denial. Her daily work schedule forced her to put one foot in front of the other as she went to meet Miss Addie in the kitchen for morning coffee.

"We'll have this place to ourselves for the next three months while Mr. and Mrs. Brown visit his folks down south," the housekeeper said. "They still need help putting things right since the war is over."

"I forgot." Annika stared into her coffee cup without looking up.

"Child, what happened to your cheek?"

"I scraped it." Annika's hand flew to her cheek to cover it. "When I fell out of bed." She pushed back her chair and set about helping Miss Addie prepare breakfast.

Annika spent the remainder of the week always alert while she helped Mrs. Brown prepare for the trip. During the day, she stayed close to either Miss Addie or Mrs. Brown and never remained in the same room with Mr. Brown. Nights were long and sleepless. Each evening, she shoved her bed against the locked door and kept Pappa's whittling knife within reach. She didn't know a word to describe her relief when the Browns left.

◆

Day after day, week after week, Annika and Miss Addie cleaned the three-story house from top to bottom, working from the list Mrs. Brown had left. Addie suggested they start with the worst job: cleaning out the root cellar located behind the back porch and beneath the servants' quarters. The dank, dingy job matched Annika's frame of mind. She drew some satisfaction when the shelves were swept clean for the fall garden produce. She could see what she had accomplished. Then they moved on to cleaning fireplace hearths that serviced every bedroom in the house, another dirty but rewarding job.

She washed and polished the beautiful native woodwork and wall coverings, but there was no feeling of satisfaction. She and Addie worked together in cleaning and organizing each room and closet. Washing windows, laundering draperies, and rehanging them concluded their list of major chores. They resumed their routine household duties, thus providing themselves with a bit of vacation. Annika used free time to work on special sewing projects. She drew great pleasure from any time spent with needle and thread.

The aroma of fresh coffee made Annika's stomach lurch. She took the tray of butter, jam, and biscuits Miss Addie had set out on the kitchen table and headed down the south hall. On Sundays, when the Browns were away, they took morning coffee in the back parlor, where Mrs. Brown read and took her afternoon tea. It was also where Mrs. Brown schooled Annika, who loved the cozy room, with its corner fireplace. While Addie filled the mugs, Annika lowered the tray to the small table between their chairs. Annika's cheeks flushed red under Miss Addie's keen gaze. Her secret burden had taken a heavy toll on her spirit.

"Only half a cup. I want more milk than coffee."

"I'm worried about you," Miss Addie said. "You are too young to have dark circles beneath your eyes. You look completely spent."

"I don't sleep." Annika self-consciously poured milk into her coffee and buttered a biscuit. She wished Miss Addie was less observant.

"Why?" Miss Addie asked.

Annika drew a deep breath and lowered her eyes. She spoke after a long silence. "I'm in trouble, and I have no one to turn to. I tried to talk to Pastor Winn two or three Sundays ago."

Miss Addie made no response.

"He thought I was going to ask for money or

something—anyway, it didn't go well. Now everyone at church is whispering and avoiding me. They know nothing about me. I won't go back."

Miss Addie sipped her coffee.

"The church, you, and Mrs. Brown are my life. I can't go to Mrs. Brown with this."

"They return next week," Miss Addie said.

"I've thought of nothing else. I feel dirty." Annika's anger smothered her will to talk, but Miss Addie's anguished expression spurred her on. "I missed my last two times of the month."

"Maybe you are ill?"

"No, three nights before they left, he came into my room—I thought I was safe." Annika's voice broke, and she sobbed.

"Oh no, I thought he had changed his ways. He's no good at all." Miss Addie gathered Annika into a motherly embrace and smoothed her hair away from her tear-streaked face. "You can't be with child. It's not fair how this calamity, this shame, comes to the woman. It's not right at all. There's no way to make this right, but I tell you Brown owes you financial help."

"Fact is I must make changes." Annika fought to regain control. "I wrote to my cousin weeks ago and told him I don't feel safe here. I asked if I could go there."

"Being with family from your country is good. I'm not visiting my daughter today—why don't we spend the day making a pie and playing cribbage?" Miss Addie said. "It will give us time to talk."

"That sounds so much better than spending the day alone." Annika attempted a faint smile. A day with a good friend was just what she needed.

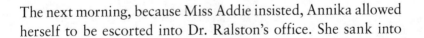

The next morning, because Miss Addie insisted, Annika allowed herself to be escorted into Dr. Ralston's office. She sank into the leather-upholstered chair beside his desk while Miss Addie waited across the room in an identical chair.

The doctor completed a brief examination and medical history before he confirmed that Annika was pregnant. He estimated the due date to be November. Annika stared at the brick wall in front of her and made no response.

"I've helped other girls in this circumstance. Marriage is always the best solution. Do you plan to marry?" he asked.

"No."

"In that case, I suggest asking for help from the New York Children's Asylum or the Children's Aid Society. Both take in wayward children."

Annika's face burned with indignation. "Because I'm not marrying, you think I'm wayward? I'm not wayward. I have a job and a place to live. I pay my way, and I will take care of this baby."

"I'm trying to save you heartache. People look down on this, you know." His tone was kinder than his words.

"I'm not happy either. How much do I owe you?" Annika asked as she stood to leave.

"My office girl will help you with that," Dr. Ralston said.

Annika didn't respond to his stunned expression as she stalked toward the door.

"Miss Svensson has family who will help her," Miss Addie said before she rose and followed Annika.

Anger and defeat burned hot as Annika debated her future. Because her cousin's response to her letter failed to arrive before the Browns returned, Annika took matters into her own hands. She stood in the main entry hall with the Browns' front parlor behind her and the front door to her right. Standing at the foot of the staircase, she faced Mr. Brown's closed study door. She knocked and entered without waiting for a response. The dark room already reeked of stale tobacco fumes, despite the recent cleaning. She left the door ajar and stood midway between his massive walnut desk and the only exit. Brown sat hunched over his desk, muttering and shuffling papers. Annika stood firm and waited for his full attention.

"What do you want?" he snarled.

"To talk. Why else would I be here?"

He looked up, their eyes met, and he looked away.

*Coward.*

Brown pushed away from the desk, leaned back in his pedestal roller chair, and leveled a withering glare. He relit his pipe. The sickening smell flooded the room.

Annika fastened her eyes to his and spoke in a calm, even tone. "I'm with child."

"Who's the father?"

"You know." Annika's teeth clenched against the rage she felt.

"How can you be so sure? A little immigrant trollop like you probably has many beaus."

"Would you rather I talk to Mrs. Brown?" Annika threw caution to the wind, forgetting Brown's threat. She curled her fingers into fists and kept a tight rein on her rage while she waited for his admission.

"I have done you no harm." Brown's puffy, round face and thick neck reddened to his shirt collar. He shoved his papers aside and cleared his throat as if to continue.

"That's a lie. All you thought about was yourself. You took what you wanted because you knew you could. Does your wife know what kind of man you really are?" Annika's voice rose.

"Can we talk about this?" Brown asked in a grandfatherly tone, apparently hoping to quell the rising fury.

"We are talking. I have set my plan. I carry the child, but you bear the burden. The guilt and shame are yours. You have a duty to this child. If you fail to meet that responsibility, I'll inform your wife of your vile actions. I want cash to make a new start and to provide an education for the child. I want hard money, not worthless greenbacks and continentals."

"You good-for-nothing little immigrant slut. Who do you think you are, talking to me like that?" He bolted from his chair, lunged across the desk, and bellowed.

Annika didn't budge. "I was a pure young girl until I came across you." She narrowed her eyes and glared back. "I'll tell your wife and anyone else who will listen if you ever come near me again. I expect the money within the week."

"I don't care what you expect, you little whore," he sputtered.

"You'd better." Annika's icy gaze cut through the void between them like a saber.

Finally, he broke eye contact and sank into his chair, mumbling to himself, obviously befuddled. Annika exited into the hallway and directly into Mrs. Brown's path. Her heart raced, and her legs shook, so Annika took a moment to summon a civil attitude before she spoke.

"I'm indebted to you for what you have done for me and my mother. I have decided to join my family in Minnesota. I will leave this job as soon as I hear from them."

"Annika, is something wrong?"

"Ask him. He's the man with the answers." Annika escaped to her room, locked the door, and collapsed into the chair without taking time to report to Addie. With trembling hand, she wrote.

New York City
May 15, 1866

Dear Noak and Kjerstin,
I will come to Minnesota on my own. I can buy
a train ticket to Minneapolis. When I get there,
I will make plans to continue on to Washington

County. I will leave as soon as I get the money.
I look forward to seeing you.

Your cousin,
Annika

◆

Annika mopped perspiration from her face with her apron. She
leaned on the hoe handle, surveyed the three rows of potatoes
she had just weeded, and then stretched her aching back muscles.

"You have company," Miss Addie said as she glanced
beyond the garden gate.

Squinting into the sun, Annika watched a tall, broad-
shouldered man in his late thirties stride up the garden path.

Miss Addie picked up the bucket of tomatoes and radishes
she had gathered and started toward the house. Miss Addie's
and the man's voices carried back.

"Is this the Brown residence?"

"Yes, sir."

"I'm Noak Andersen. I have come to see Annika Svensson."

Without answering, Miss Addie hurried back to Annika.
"He's your cousin," she said.

The women walked back together. Annika hung the hoe on
the garden fence, and Miss Addie went inside.

"Hello. I'm Annika." She extended her hand. "Did you get
my letter that I was coming on my own?"

"No. When Kjerstin and I got your letter about not feeling
safe, we decided I should come."

Annika fretted about exactly what she had written in that
letter. She had been so distressed at the time that she simply
couldn't remember.

When Annika made no response, Noak continued. "I'm
sorry about your loss. I wrote to family back home."

"Thank you. I cannot stay here. I must make a new start. I
have expense money. Will we travel by train?"

"Yes, partway. I hope to go tomorrow. Can you be ready by then?"

"I'm already packed."

"You can go now?"

"I'll get my things and say goodbye." Annika led Noak along the path to the house and directed him to the freshly whitewashed yard chairs. "Wait here in the shade, and I'll bring you a cool drink." She met Miss Addie coming with a pitcher of lemonade and a plate of honey biscuits. "Will you wait with Noak until I get back?"

Annika dashed to her room and slipped into the clothing she had laid out for the trip. She checked the coins in her pocket purse and fastened it around her waist. She tucked the last of her personal items into her carrying case. When she was satisfied she had everything, she splashed her face with water but didn't take time to rebraid her hair.

She dragged the trunk down the back hallway, left it by the back door, and rested her smaller bag on top. She found Mrs. Brown reading in the parlor.

"My cousin has come, and I'm leaving."

The two women faced each other. An awkward, unspoken truth bound them.

"You've made the right decision, child. Your place is with family." The dour foreboding reflected in Mrs. Brown's eyes made Annika's heart ache.

"I wish things were different," Annika said.

"Don't we all?" Mrs. Brown picked up an envelope from her desk. "This letter of reference will help you get work." She rested a hand on Annika's shoulder for a moment.

"Thank you. I would not have survived Mamma's death without you." Annika's voice quavered.

Mrs. Brown looked away and then reached for her book.

The empty hallway returned Annika to her baggage and the door. She slipped the envelope into her bag and carried the bag in one hand and dragged the small trunk outside.

"I'll take these to the carriage and wait there," Noak said.

"Everything is happening so fast," Annika said, turning to Miss Addie.

"Mrs. Brown is going to hire a butler, and she gave me a raise," Miss Addie said.

"She's hurting—I saw it in her eyes." Annika sighed. "At least I can leave." She grasped Miss Addie's hands in hers. "I wish you the best in life. Thank you for believing in me. I will hold you in my heart always."

They hugged, and Annika walked away.

## CHAPTER 2

# THE JOURNEY

Annika settled back in the carriage seat across from Noak and waited for her thumping heart to quiet. *Finally, I'm away from that evil man.*

"We were worried when you wrote about not feeling safe. I hope you have not been harmed."

"I'm better already," Annika said. "I've lost family, home, and friends. I cannot bear the thought of losing one more thing."

A terrifying thought gripped her. She had been so intent on getting away from Brown that she had given no thought to what Minnesota held in store. *Oh well. Let tomorrow take care of itself,* she decided. Now she wanted to avoid further questioning. "Tell me about your family," Annika said.

"Kjerstin is looking forward to the company of another woman. She gets lonely out in the sticks with just us."

"What do you mean *sticks?*"

"Our cabin is surrounded by woods."

"That sounds different."

When Annika made no further comment, Noak continued. "My son, Tyko, is age ten. He's strong, and he thinks he can do a man's work. Kia is age six and timid. Both have Kjerstin's comely appearance. Maybe we can get a train from New York tonight."

"That would be good." Annika took coins from her pocket purse. "I wish to pay for our traveling expenses. Would you handle the money?" She gave Noak six twenty-dollar gold pieces.

"Where did you get such money?" Noak asked before he put the coins in his pocket.

"It's a long story."

The driver yanked the horses to a stop outside the St. Nicholas Hotel and unloaded their baggage. Annika made no further comment, although Noak's expression told her he was dissatisfied with her evasive answer. What would he have thought if he'd known about the money sewn into the folds of her petticoat? She had heard that westbound trains got robbed. Her future depended upon that money and Noak and his family. She could lose neither to a thief.

She knew Noak deserved a better answer, but she couldn't confide something so personal to someone she barely knew. Still, guilt nagged because she knew honesty, even in the worst of circumstances, was best. She would tell them, but she had no idea when or how.

Annika's eyes traveled the full length of the building and then up the multiple floors. When she and Mamma had lived in the city, she had passed by this hotel often, without ever daring to peek inside. Now she followed Noak inside as if she belonged there.

The clerk, a man with bushy eyebrows and an exacting mind, told them the next train for Chicago left in precisely two hours and fourteen minutes. One ticket would cover charges for several different lines they would travel, and that would save both time and money.

"Chicago fare for two is forty dollars, and continuing on to Rock Island, Illinois, makes the total forty-six dollars—that's about three cents a mile," he said.

They refused additional charges for seats that converted to sleeping berths or a private compartment. Annika did not wish to lie down among strangers.

"The conductor can change your accommodations en route," the clerk told them. As the men completed their transaction, the clerk advised that the café next door put out a good meal and prepared food baskets for travelers. He suggested they leave their baggage with him.

Pink tinged Annika's cheeks as Noak escorted her into the café and helped her with her chair. Never had she been treated with such consideration. It was midafternoon, and the café was nearly empty.

When their fried chicken, potatoes, and carrots arrived, they ate with hearty appetites.

"Chicago will be about halfway home," Noak said. "Coming here was much easier than our first trip out to Minnesota. Everyone who sailed with us rode in a converted cattle wagon they called an immigrant car—at least the price was right."

The waitress refilled their coffee cups, and Noak ordered a food basket for two people for three days. Annika watched Noak receive change from a ten-dollar gold piece.

The screech of a whistle startled Annika. "That is our train. We must hurry."

They retrieved their baggage and went directly to the baggage master to check it. The line was long. Annika watched Noak take a short length of rope from his own bag, and then he placed their smaller bags on top of Annika's trunk and looped the rope through the handles of each bag and the trunk handles, binding the three into a single unit. She wondered what he was doing.

"Now they will not get separated," Noak told Annika. He told the baggage master their destination, and the man secured a large, diamond-shaped brass check to the rope that bound their baggage. He handed Noak a duplicate as a receipt. *Rock Island* was stamped on each tag.

They made their way to the railcar reserved for ladies traveling with gentlemen. Annika climbed the steep steps and stopped in the doorway until her eyes adjusted to the dim light. The car was plain, with a narrow center aisle that extended the length of the car and ended with a closed door. Pew-like seats wide enough to seat two were grouped along each side of the aisle. The seats faced each other in pairs and permitted four people to sit together and visit. The car was about half filled with passengers. There was a ladies' room at one end of the car, with a men's room at the opposite end.

Annika couldn't resist smiling at a perky red-haired girl who sat with several other children and four adults at the far end of the car. Annika selected an aisle seat toward the middle of the car, facing the children.

"The middle seats are supposed to be safer, though I doubt any seat is safe if the train derails," Noak said.

Annika shuddered when she noticed some men board the train with guns. She distracted herself by asking Noak, "How fast does this thing go?"

"I've heard they cover anywhere from twenty to forty miles in an hour. They go slower at night."

Annika wanted the train to get underway. Finally, she heard, "All aboard," and watched the conductor wave to the engineer. The train jolted forward. Dust and smoke irritated her throat, and she could taste the grit in the air.

The commotion disturbed the children, but Annika barely noticed. She slid toward the window and looked outside. The train rushed in a general northwesterly direction, leaving the city behind. Annika had never been outside the city, and she was curious to see the open spaces filled with trees, fences, and farm animals.

The view had become monotonous by the time daylight faded.

Annika slumped back against her seat and let her thoughts wander. Noak dozed. She fretted about her situation. How could it be God's will that she was orphaned and pregnant? She found no answer but knew Brown, not God, was responsible for her hateful circumstances. She had to leave New York. She couldn't allow that doctor to send her away to an asylum. Her parents had brought her to North America to be free. She drifted to sleep.

When she awoke, it was pitch black outside. Candles along the walls of the car provided only dim light. She felt as if she had become part of the seat in which she sat. Her dress clung to the seat when she shifted positions. Across the aisle, a man slept with his shoeless feet sticking out an open window. The young travelers were quiet. Some of the small children cuddled on the laps of adults, while the older children dozed in whatever space they could claim. Annika wondered why the children wore tags sewn onto the front of their clothing. Each tag had either a number or a word written on it. No one had given her a tag.

She stood and gripped the metal frame of the seat until she gained her balance. Then she moved toward the ladies' room. An offensive stench caused her to draw a deep breath before she entered and quickly took care of her business. She washed her hands and dried them on her handkerchief. She dampened the cloth, wrung it out, and tucked it into the neck of her dress to cool herself.

The railcar took a hard jolt to the left, and she stumbled. Feeling faint, she inched her way back to her seat. When the feeling failed to pass, she decided to eat something. She retrieved a small chunk of cheese from the food basket before realizing she had company. The little red-haired girl had slipped into the seat across from her. Annika broke the cheese and handed the child a piece.

"Thank you. I am seven years old," the girl said with a thick Irish brogue.

"I'm fourteen." Annika watched a maternal-looking middle-aged woman scurry toward them.

"Kathleen, you know it's against the rules to talk to people you don't know, much less beg food." The woman turned to Annika and smiled. "I apologize. We do feed the children. I'm afraid Kathleen is a restless sleeper."

"I gave her the cheese. Why does she wear the Chicago tag?"

"She is going to Chicago to meet her new parents." The woman took Kathleen's hand and led her away.

◆

Annika narrowed her eyes against the reflection of the sun on the surface of Lake Erie as the train skirted the southern shoreline. A breeze blew in and refreshed her.

Later, Annika walked about and stretched her legs when the train stopped to take on water and wood in rural Indiana. The building, like most of the other rural depots had been, was a drab, cheerless wooden structure. Suddenly, Annika caught a glimpse of a red head disappearing behind the shed. She whirled, quickly surveyed the group of children, and realized Kathleen was nowhere in sight. Annika bolted toward the exit and bumped into Noak.

"I'll be right back. Don't let them leave without me. I think Kathleen is running away."

Annika clung to the support bar and flung herself down the steps, and within seconds, she was behind the depot. She found Kathleen cowering between a large rain barrel and the back wall of the depot, nearly concealed in shadows.

"Kathleen, what is wrong?"

"Leave me alone. I'm going to New York to find my mother. I don't want to live in Chicago."

"I'm worried. How will you find your way back to New York?"

Kathleen refused to budge.

"Please come out and talk to me." Annika reached out a hand to welcome the child.

"I'm scared." Kathleen stepped out, threw her arms around Annika, and sobbed.

"All aboard. All aboard."

The train whistle echoed in Annika's ears. She grasped Kathleen's hand and towed her toward the train.

"You and I are alike. You are starting a new life in Chicago, and I'm starting a new life in Minnesota—that is even farther away than Chicago. Just like you, I don't know the people I'll be living with either."

The woman from the night before and the conductor greeted them with grim faces. Annika hoisted Kathleen into the woman's arms. She felt the ground slide from under her foot as she lifted it onto the bottom step. The train was on its way. The firm grip on Annika's arm frightened her until she realized the conductor was merely safeguarding her boarding.

"Are you hurt?" Noak asked as he took her arm and escorted her to their seats. Kathleen and the woman were nowhere in sight. "What happened?"

"I was afraid that little girl would be left behind. So I went after her. She was running away." Annika, who was out of breath and thirsty, welcomed Noak's suggestion that they eat.

"Allow me to introduce myself." The man who spoke wore a navy-blue business suit. "I'm Charles Loring Brace with the Children's Aid Society." He extended a hand to Noak.

Noak stood and grasped his hand as he introduced himself and Annika and then invited the man to sit with them.

"Thank you for what you did," Brace told Annika. "You are to be commended. Not all people are willing to extend themselves to help others." Turning to Noak, he added, "You have reason to be proud of this young lady."

Noak smiled.

"I'm afraid for Kathleen," Annika said. "She wanted to run away to New York City to find her mother."

"She has been with us for three years, and we have had no contact with either parent. We are trying to give her a new start in a better situation."

"I tried to encourage her. I hope she isn't angry."

"You did the right thing." Brace rose, nodded amiably, and returned to his charges.

"What is the Children's Aid Society?" Noak asked.

"It's a home for children whose parents are either dead or

too poor to care for their children. In New York City, there are many abandoned children without homes. Reverend Brace is trying to change that by taking children out west to new homes. Mrs. Brown makes donations to the group and works there as a volunteer. She talked to me about going there when Mamma passed, but I wanted to stay and work for her."

"I had no idea."

The train pulled into Chicago the next morning. Annika watched as the orphan train riders marched down the aisle of the railcar to their unknown futures.

"I'll miss you," Kathleen whispered to Annika as she passed by.

Annika squeezed the child's hand and gave her a "Be brave" smile.

Annika and Noak followed the tantalizing aroma of coffee to the depot's food bar.

"Our stop at Rock Island brings us to the Mississippi River and the last leg of our trip," Noak said. "We could take the train to St. Paul, but that is too far west, so we'll book a steamboat and travel north up the Mississippi to the St. Croix River."

"How long is the trip to Rock Island?"

"If all goes well, five hours," Noak said.

They ate a hot breakfast and waited while the cook packed their food basket with beef sandwiches, apples, water, an orange, and two peppermint sticks. They paid and weaved their way through the crowded depot and back to their coach. En route, Annika glimpsed Kathleen on the far side of the station, walking with a young couple and clutching a baby doll. She smiled.

Annika, weary from being confined to a passenger car, was relieved when the train pulled into the Rock Island station. She and Noak went directly to the baggage master and claimed their possessions. Noak located a dockworker, who agreed to transport them to the pier in exchange for Noak's help in unloading freight. Annika sat in the shade and watched.

"I'm going to speak to the harbormaster to see if the *Viola* is docked," the freight handler told them when they arrived at the dock. "Will you wait with the freight?"

"Yes," Noak answered.

"I'm thankful I didn't try this trip on my own," Annika said. "When I get to Minnesota, I plan to stay put."

Noak chuckled.

"The *Viola* ain't in dock, and they don't know if she's going to come. I got to find another freighter. The harbormaster says a St. Louis steamer captain in dock is looking to increase his load," the man said. "I've got orders: if the *Viola* ain't in sight, I'm to put this freight on the first available steamer to St. Paul. These shippers want to work with established lines they can depend upon. I've got to make the arrangements."

Annika hated waiting alone with the freight wagon while the men went aboard to talk to the ship's clerk. She felt out of place amid the shouting and hollering. She wondered about the destinations of the boxes, barrels, and bags the men rousted. The thought of trying to keep the cargo straight made her head ache.

"I booked deck passage on this steamer," Noak told her. "Their cabins were full. We can make connections with the *Viola* in Wisconsin, at La Crosse or Prescott."

"What is deck passage?"

"It's transport only. Maybe we can follow this freight aboard and use it to arrange benches or beds," Noak said. He picked up their bundle and started up the gangplank. Annika followed with the food basket.

"I see you made it aboard," a young man said.

"Yes," Annika replied without pausing.

Noak gave the man a suspicious look and continued arranging crates into seats with back supports.

Annika took stock of her strange surroundings, with cargo and penned-in cattle in close proximity. She was frightened about the deck passage, and she was hot, dirty, and physically drained. She sank onto a nearby crate. Never had she imagined a trip like this one. August heat sapped her energy, and she was hungry again.

"We can use this as a table," Noak said as he turned the trunk onto its side and slid it in front of Annika.

"I'm hungry," Annika said, reaching for the food basket. "Are you ready to eat?" Not waiting for an answer, she spread a cloth over the trunk and set out the water jug, apples, sandwiches, and a thick slice of cheese, which she bent until it broke.

"Who was that young man?" Noak asked as he set the water jug back on the trunk.

"I think he works on this ship. When I waited with the freight, he called to me and asked if I needed help loading."

"Maybe he thinks you are pretty. Women are scarce out here. We will have many callers when word gets around the territory that there is a new young lady at our place."

"Oh no, I have never received a caller. I'm not ready." Annika blushed scarlet.

"Sometimes men can be a trifle forward."

Annika tidied up after their meal and walked over to the guardrail. She inhaled fresh, clean air. A thick, lush canopy of green trees covered the opposite bank. Annika wanted to trust the tranquility, but she knew better.

"Do you know you are beautiful?" a masculine voice asked.

Annika stiffened and stepped away.

"I just want to talk. I don't see many people my age on this tub," the wiry young man with unkempt blond hair said.

"You startled me. Are you one of the crew?"

"You might say that. I'm working my passage to St. Paul,

Minnesota. I'm putting Missouri behind me as fast as I can. I'm not in any trouble, mind you. I'm just making a new start."

"Are you from Missouri?"

"No, New Jersey. The orphan train brought me to Missouri five years ago." He paused and gazed across the water. "My host parents weren't the kind of people I wanted to stay around. I tried to fight for the North when I was sixteen, but they wouldn't let me enlist. On my eighteenth birthday, I left."

"I met an orphan child who was being placed in Chicago. I saw her leaving the depot with her new parents. I hope everything goes well for her."

"Don't worry. Most of the children I came out with got along well. It was just that my parents were mean folks who were looking for free labor."

Annika turned in response to a gentle tap on her shoulder and found Noak a half step behind them.

"I thought I would introduce myself to your friend."

"Yes, sir, I'm Willie Barnes. We are passing the time of day. I don't see many people my age out here. It gets lonely, you know." They shook hands.

"I'm Noak Andersen, and this attractive young lady who has caught your eye is my goddaughter, Annika Svensson."

"I'm pleased to meet you both," Willie said.

A voice from nowhere called out, "Willie!"

Willie excused himself, and Noak and Annika watched him trot away.

"He came out here on the orphan train but left his new parents when he turned eighteen, because they were mean," Annika said. "I'm thankful I have family."

Annika and Noak returned to their camp area and settled in for the trip.

An ear-splitting blast of the steam whistle announced a change in the steamer's course.

"No cause for alarm," Noak told Annika. "We're approaching La Crosse, Wisconsin. The clerk told me there would be a brief stop to unload freight and take on more wood. I'm going to help haul fuel wood. You might as well try to get some rest. Our last stop will be Prescott, at the confluence of the Mississippi and St. Croix rivers. Captain Knapp should have the *Viola* in port there."

Later that day, the steamer docked in Prescott, and Annika waited on board while Noak made arrangements for passage up the St. Croix River. She felt ill at ease in this unknown territory as she stood vigil on the deck and waited. Her spirits lifted as she watched Noak stride back toward the steamer. *Good. Everything will be all right.*

"I booked double-berth cabin passage, and we can stay there tonight. The *Viola* has been in port a couple of days and will launch early tomorrow. By evening, we should be in Stillwater, Minnesota, almost home."

They gathered their possessions and started down the gangplank but paused when someone approached.

"I wanted to tell you folks goodbye. Hope your trip is safe and uneventful." Willie spoke to Noak, but his eyes rested on Annika, who responded with a shy smile.

The men shook hands, Annika wished Willie a safe trip also, and she and Noak continued on their way.

Annika felt dwarfed standing in the shadow of the *Viola*, even though it was a smaller steamer than the previous ship. It must have been more than one hundred feet long, with its water wheel mounted on the side instead of at the rear of the craft.

"This steamer was built in Franconia, a town about ten miles north of Marine Settlement, where we live," Noak said.

They located their cabin on the west side of the upper deck, dropped off their belongings, and locked the door. Following Captain Knapp's directions, they headed toward State Street, where they expected to find an open café.

Annika sank into a chair, thankful to be away from water.

The waitress served each a glass of milk and a bowl of venison stew with potatoes, green beans, and hot biscuits. Annika was famished, and the hot meal was satisfying.

"If you think this is good, wait until you taste Kjerstin's stew. She is one of the best cooks in the entire territory," Noak said.

Annika smiled and continued eating.

They took their time in returning to the *Viola*.

"You showed pioneer spirit last night, sleeping under the stars. That couldn't have been easy for a city girl," Noak said.

"I didn't sleep much," Annika confessed. There was no need to tell Noak how frightened and uncomfortable she had felt. "I'm looking forward to privacy and a bed."

"I don't know about you, but I want to clean up. I hate to think how long I have been wearing these clothes," Noak said.

Back on board, Annika searched out the ladies' room. When she returned, she found Noak stretched out on his berth.

She lay down, overcome with fatigue. Her body rested, but her thoughts churned. This land was raw with an energy that ignited everything. Yet Noak went from task to task, taking every challenge in stride. She was safe with Noak.

Annika took a clean, wrinkled shirtwaist dress from her bag and flipped it several times. She laid it on the bed and smoothed away the wrinkles the best she could with her hands.

"I'm going to have a look around while you freshen up. Then you can return the favor," Noak said.

Annika stepped over and locked the door. She took off her shoes and dress and checked the money sewn into her petticoat. She poured water into the washbasin and wet a clean washcloth. There was no soap. She washed her face, taking time to enjoy the refreshing feeling. She washed her hands, arms, legs, and feet and toweled dry. She donned the fresh dress and unbraided her hair. She brushed her hair vigorously and decided to relax for a few minutes before signaling Noak—instead, she drifted to sleep. She didn't stir until she heard Noak's knock at the door.

Instantly awake, she rushed to the door to admit him. "I'm sorry. I dozed off," Annika said. "I'll let you have your time."

◆

Annika and Noak slept through breakfast the next morning. The *Viola* was well on its way by the time Annika strolled to the dining room to meet Noak for the noon meal. She was surprised to find the food already on the tables, waiting for guests to arrive. Noak visited with two men at their table. Annika ate quickly, excused herself, and went back to the cabin. She was still tired, and the table manners of some diners annoyed her. Annika slept for another three hours and awoke feeling renewed.

She joined Noak, who leaned against the guardrail on the main deck. He identified points of interest along the way, but mostly, they floated along silently, each thinking their own thoughts.

Annika couldn't even think about confiding in Noak without her chest tightening. Fear overwhelmed her.

"I have something to say, though I'm unsure how it will be received." Noak established eye contact with Annika and then rested his eyes on the northern horizon. "I was honored when your parents asked me to be your godparent. When I affirmed that commitment at your christening, I was sincere. I knew responsibility came with the privilege." He paused for several moments.

Annika's heart pounded, and her thoughts darted about. *Does he know? Did Miss Addie tell him? What is going to happen?* She gripped the handrail with the strength of someone expecting to be thrown overboard. She struggled to contain her emotions and focus upon what the man was saying.

"Your actions show you are a good and honest person. Kjerstin and I believe that God has brought you into our lives for his own purpose. We want you to become part of our family.

I hope, with time, you will trust us as you would your own parents."

Annika touched his arm with a tentative hand as she pushed back tears that threatened to betray her secret. They continued their journey.

## CHAPTER 3

# THE ARRIVAL

Noak pointed toward a clump of houses and buildings huddled along the shoreline. "That's Stillwater, the county seat for Washington County," he said.

Annika envied his anticipation. Her shoulders ached, and her chest was tight. Quick, shallow breaths left her needing more air. She tried to breathe normally, but her heart pounded. Minnesota was her only option, and she had to make it work.

"Are you feeling ill?" Noak asked as they strolled back to the cabin.

"I feel like Kathleen must have felt," Annika said with a shaky smile.

Inside the cabin, Annika brushed her hair, gathered it at the crown of her head, and coiled it into a bun. She anchored it with hair combs and tucked her brush into her bag. When she bent to pick up the food basket, dizziness overtook her. Moments later, her limp body was suspended in midair, being carried to the bunk. Murky gray engulfed her. The roar in her ears made her head ache.

"Are you all right? Can you hear me?" a familiar voice asked.

She tried to sit up, but someone—*Oh, it's Noak*—restrained her.

"Please lie quietly."

"I'm fine. I'm fine," she said as she complied and closed her eyes just as Captain Knapp appeared in the cabin doorway.

"Is there anything I can do? I was told we had sickness in this cabin," the captain said.

Noak walked across the room before he spoke. "Yes. She fainted. She's pale but says she's fine. I think we'll stop by the doctor's house in Stillwater."

"I reckon you know where he lives?"

"Yes. Thank you for your concern." Noak extended a hand. "It was good to see you again, old friend."

"Yes, it was good to see you too." Captain Knapp grinned. "If all's well, I'll get back to the business of docking."

Fear mounted. Annika drew deep, even breaths. Knowing that her mother had fainted when she was pregnant offered no solace. Noak brought her a cool dipper of water and kept watch nearby. He appeared uncomfortable and unsure. She feigned sleeping until she heard Noak leave.

The sounds of scurrying about on deck and the steamer's whistle alerted Annika that the *Viola* was docking. She sat up, swung her feet to the floor, and smoothed her hair.

"I feel much better," she responded to Noak's unspoken question when he returned.

"Shall we go ashore then?" he asked.

They toted their cargo toward the gangplank.

The northwest horizon revealed businesses and homes situated at the base and along the steep bluffs rising on three sides. Late-afternoon sun spilled across the deck, and balmy air buffed pink into Annika's cheeks. Upstream, tree-sized logs floated in slow-moving current along a shoreline cluttered with saw mills, logs, and storage sheds. Noak and Annika left the steamer and made their way up the incline to a main street that ran parallel to the river. The town was quiet, and so were Annika and Noak. Sawdust and pine needles covered the boardwalk along the St. Croix riverfront and identified the place as a logging town. A lone carriage here and there testified that it was Sunday.

"I want you to see the doctor," Noak said.

"But I'm feeling fine now. I got dizzy and maybe scared—that's all."

"Just the same, I'd feel better if Dr. Randall examined you. Our cabin is too far out to make the trip twice."

"Oh." Annika breathed deeply and slowly and tried to remain calm. She couldn't risk fainting again.

"Noak, you're back!" a robust voice called.

Noak lowered the trunk to the ground, and they waited in the shade of a large oak near a closed blacksmith shop. Annika searched the vicinity for the owner of the voice and spied a two-seat buggy approaching. The driver pulled to the side of the street and helped a young girl down. The girl hooked her arm into his and hastened her steps to keep pace with the young man's long strides. Her skirt ruffled the sawdust as she walked. Noak smiled and greeted them as friends.

"We just docked. This is my cousin's daughter, Annika Svensson. This is Oscar Carlsson and his friend Lota Robinson."

The young woman was small in stature, with wavy chestnut hair tied in green ribbons that accented her beautiful eyes.

"Welcome to Minnesota." Oscar touched the brim of his hat and nodded. His somber gray eyes met Annika's uplifted gaze. His closely trimmed dark mustache stopped at the corners of his mouth. She knew he couldn't have been more than twenty-four years old.

"Hello," Lota said in a wispy, breathy voice.

"It's good to meet you." Annika used her politest smile.

"Where are you headed?" Oscar asked.

"To the doctor's house," Noak said. "Then we'll get a room and start for home in the morning."

"I'm headed there after I take Lota home. You're welcome to ride along."

"What do you think?" Noak looked to Annika.

"The sooner we get there, the sooner I can stay put," Annika said.

Lota inched closer to Oscar.

31

"Let's stow the bags." Oscar lifted Lota's hand from his arm, grasped one handle of the trunk, and gathered the food basket in his other hand. Lota and Annika watched the men deposit the bundles in the rear seat of the buggy.

"Have you lived in Stillwater long?" Annika asked Lota.

"We've been here two years. My father owns the store." Lota eyed Annika from head to toe. "How long do you expect to visit?"

"I hope to make this my home if all goes well." Annika felt uneasy under Lota's critical eye. Her hands fluttered nervously until she decided to hook a thumb into the waistband of her pocket purse.

"You look exhausted," Lota said, shaking her head and clicking her tongue as if she were scolding a child.

Annika resented her attitude. "I am tired. It's been a long trip."

"Where are you from?"

"I'm from Sweden, but I've been living in New York City for the last eight years. My mother was pregnant and unable to continue the trip to Minnesota, so we settled there for a while."

"New York City must be huge."

"Yes, but I didn't see much of downtown after I went to work as a domestic for a wealthy family who lived on the edge of the city limits."

"I've been working as a clerk three days a week up there. See the Stillwater Mercantile sign?" Lota pointed up the street to a large storefront across from them. "I'm going to teach at the Hay Lake School this year and live in a boardinghouse near there. If I like it, I'll apply for teaching certification next summer. I'm looking forward to spending more time with Oscar." Lota's eyes drifted to Oscar, whose chuckle made her smile. She turned back to Annika. "We keep company on Sundays. Today we went to the church my family attends, and his parents invited us for dinner."

Annika didn't respond, and Lota turned on her heel and flounced away to join Oscar.

"I'll take Lota home and meet you at Doc's," Oscar said as he clapped Noak on the back. He looked past Lota and nodded to Annika, whose stomach fluttered.

Lota tossed her long, wavy tresses over her shoulder and looked away. She hooked her arm in Oscar's and moved toward the front seat of the buggy.

"Dr. Randall's place is up here," Noak said. "How are you feeling?"

"Fine. I don't think Lota liked me much," Annika said, changing the subject.

"Pay her no mind. She's sweet on Oscar. Most young women in these parts are married or spoken for by the time they reach Lota's age. Maybe she's afraid you'll steal her beau."

They passed the store Lota had pointed out, other businesses, and a newspaper office with *Stillwater Messenger* painted on the front window.

"You and Oscar are friends?" Annika asked.

"I work in the timber with him in the winter when money is scarce. His father operates the Stillwater Lumber Company, and Oscar runs their winter camp. He also farms."

Annika remembered the often-told story of the family's original immigration plans. Her father and Noak had planned to file squatters' claims on adjacent properties, form a partnership, and increase their prospect of success. That was why her *far* had sent his tools along to Minnesota when their family stayed behind in New York.

"Was it hard to start out on your own without Pappa?" Annika asked.

"I was able to stake claim on one hundred sixty acres surrounded by open territory I hoped your father could claim when he arrived. The first year was tough. We had to build a house and begin clearing the land for cultivation. We've been settled for more than five years, and the homestead is ours. It's a hard life but a good life."

"Is Oscar's farm near yours?"

"He lives over by Hay Lake and is one of our closer neighbors. He had it a little easier. When the Homestead Act of 1862 was enacted, he was able to get a clear title to his Hay Lake property after only six months of homesteading and paying a dollar and a quarter per acre. When our families lost touch, Oscar and I took up a partnership agreement with the understanding that Tomas would join us when he arrived."

"That explains why he was so happy to see you," Annika said with a smile.

"Kjerstin and Oscar's wife were good friends. But Oscar lost both his wife and their baby in childbirth about two years ago."

Annika gasped and fell silent.

"Here we are." Noak rapped on the door. "Is Dr. Randall home? I'd like him to check my goddaughter. She fainted earlier today," he told the short, plump woman who opened the door.

"Come in and have a seat, and I'll fetch you a drink of water." She motioned toward two hallway chairs and continued toward the back of the house. She returned, handed each a glass of water, and said, "My husband was called to Taylors Falls late yesterday. He's not back. Is this serious?"

"No." Annika spoke up. "I got dizzy. I'm tired. We've come all the way from New York City."

"That's quite a trip." She touched Annika's forehead with a small, cool palm and then felt her pulse. "Do you have pain or discomfort?"

"No, I feel fine."

The woman excused herself and answered a knock at the door. "Oscar, come in. Today is the day for callers."

"Good evening, Sarah. How are you?" Oscar asked. "I've come for your callers so we can head home."

"Oh, you're not staying with your parents tonight?"

"No, I've got work to see to," Oscar said as they joined Noak and Annika.

"Maybe it is fatigue," Noak said.

"You're welcome to check back in a day or two if you're still concerned," Sarah said.

"Thank you. I'm sure I'll be fine," Annika said.

Outside, as Annika climbed into the buggy, she felt her feet leave the ground, and straightaway, with a gentle plop, she was seated next to her luggage. Oscar smiled. Annika, disarmed by his casual charm, felt a flutter again. She resisted the urge to smile. *Maybe Lota has reason to be touchy*, Annika told herself. *If that is the case, she need not worry about me.*

The men clambered into the front seat, and Oscar reined the horse to the north and launched into the latest news.

The road away from Stillwater was well traveled as it wound along the banks of the St. Croix River. Annika heard bits and pieces of the men's conversation. Oscar had been looking in on Kjerstin and the children. When he'd heard the *Viola* whistle its approach, he had driven through town, thinking Noak might be aboard.

Annika turned to her own thoughts. She hoped the homestead wasn't much farther. The road narrowed as they turned left into timber so thick the setting sun seldom broke through. She recognized a faint aroma of blueberries wafting from the woods. Birds, squirrels, and creatures Annika couldn't identify filled the trees. She fretted about bears, wolves, and Indians. The lumpy ride kept her alert. What a relief the doctor had been away. She hadn't wanted to go near him, but she could not refuse Noak. He meant well. She battled with herself. Which was worse: bearing the shame she hid or enduring the guilt of being dishonest?

"There's Hay Lake," Annika heard Oscar say. "You could drop me by my place and take the buggy, and I'll pick it up the first of the week. Or you could spend the night and go home tomorrow."

"I can't stay over when we are so close," Noak said as a slight jolt told Annika they were veering to the right. "I've been missing Kjerstin and the little ones. I'll take the rig if you agree to come for a meal tomorrow."

"I never pass up an invitation to share Kjerstin's fixings."

Annika sensed a strong bond between the men. She hoped for a connection like that with the Andersens and friends of her own.

"It was a pleasure to make your acquaintance," Oscar told Annika. Turning to Noak, he asked, "Are you sure you don't want a break before you continue on?"

Noak declined Oscar's inquiry, and within minutes, he and Annika were back on their way.

"We're less than an hour from home," Noak said. "How are you doing?"

"I can handle that." Annika yawned.

"This road leads to the farm." Noak reined the horse to the right and onto a road barely the width of a wagon. The darkness and the woods intimidated Annika. Noak's presence reassured her.

"Looks like Kjerstin has a light in the window. Tyko and Kia are in bed by now," Noak said as he pointed ahead and to the left. "This cabin is much warmer than our first one. I have inside work to finish, but I'll do that this winter, if we have a good crop."

"You built it yourself?" Annika asked.

"I felled the trees, cut the logs, stripped the bark from them so they could dry, and split the shakes. That took quite a long time. Oscar and men from church helped timber it up."

"Do you have a barn?"

"I dug into a hill above the lake and reinforced the three earth sides with timber, built stalls, and enclosed the front. That's where we sheltered our cow and a couple of chickens. Above the stable, I built a rough one-room cabin and fireplace. Our first winter was severe. We lived there for about five years until the new cabin was finished. Now the first place is our feed storage and work shed."

"I hope I don't crowd everyone."

"The cabin is plenty big. When we got Emelie's letter, I got busy and finished the loft. I'm sure Kjerstin will show you around tomorrow."

The buggy rolled into a clearing. The road hugged the crest of the rise, and their cabin overlooked a small lake on Annika's right. Moonlight gleamed on the water and illuminated the fence along the road.

"I haven't seen fences like that since I left Sweden. Why do Swedes build fences like that?" Annika asked.

"We built that one to remind us of home," Noak said. "Back home, there was so little topsoil on the rock base that we couldn't sink posts deep enough to hold fence rail. So we set double posts and secured slanting rails between each set of double posts. Slanting the horizontal rails downward lets the rain and snow drip away so the fence lasts longer. Fences like that aren't necessary here." Noak reined the horse to the left, toward the cabin door.

The door flung open. Noak bounded from the seat, flipped the reins around the hitching post, and wrapped his wife in his arms. Kjerstin was a tall, substantial-looking woman even in her faded blue nightdress. She had freshly brushed hair and greeted Noak with a kiss.

*Family*, Annika thought. She slid across the seat, climbed from the buggy, and watched the couple drift toward her hand in hand.

"How you've grown!" Kjerstin stretched an arm around Annika's shoulders and hugged her.

Annika melted into the embrace. Noak smiled and handed Kjerstin the food basket. He hoisted the trunk and bags from the buggy and followed the women inside.

"I'm going to tend to the horse." Noak took a match from the shelf above the stove, lifted a lantern from a nail by the door, and lit the wick. He carried the lantern outside, whistling as he went.

"You favor your mother, especially with your hair like that." Kjerstin pulled a chair away from the table and motioned for Annika to sit.

"I must look a sight." Annika's hand self-consciously went to her hair and confirmed that her once smooth bun was now unkempt and askew. Kjerstin smiled, and Annika giggled.

"I had a feeling you would come in today. It's a relief to have everyone home safe. Was it a terribly long trip?" Kjerstin asked. She continued without waiting for a response. "Are you hungry?" She brought the butter bowl and a loaf of bread to the table and began slicing.

"I'm more tired than hungry," Annika said, stifling a yawn. "The bread does look tasty. Noak bragged to me about your cooking. I'm so thankful he came when he did. I don't know if I could have completed the trip on my own. I hope his being gone wasn't a hardship."

"Don't fret now." Kjerstin spoke in Swedish with a sprinkling of English.

"I don't want to be a burden."

"Family takes care of family. That's why God gave us one another. What would you like to drink?" Kjerstin asked as she handed a thick slice of bread to Annika.

"If ever I needed family, it is now." Tears welled in Annika's eyes, but she refused to let them escape. "A small glass of milk would be wonderful, if you have any." Annika cut the bread in half and buttered one piece. "This is good," she said, quashing another yawn.

Noak returned and sat down behind two slices of buttered bread and a large glass of milk. "There are two peppermint sticks in the food basket. Annika wanted to bring the children a treat. If it's still good, I got you an orange," he said.

Annika finished her last bite of bread and emptied her glass.

"I love oranges," Kjerstin said as she went to check the

contents of the food basket. "Look at that child asleep on her feet, and I'm prattling on, thinking only of my orange." She went to Annika and lovingly patted her shoulder. "Come along. We'll get you settled in." Calling over her shoulder, Kjerstin told Noak, "I'll be back shortly."

Noak grinned and pushed back his chair to take off his boots.

"For tonight, you can sleep with Kia. I warned her she might awake one morning with company in bed with her. I'm not sure who is more excited about you coming—her or me." Kjerstin spoke in hushed tones as they entered the sleeping area.

"Would you think I was terrible if I slept in my petticoat?" Annika asked.

"Of course not. Can I help you get your dress off?"

"No, I've kept you from Noak too long. Go enjoy his company and your orange," Annika said. She was sound asleep as soon as her head touched the pillow.

# CHAPTER 4

# FRONTIER HOMESTEAD

Annika lay in bed surrounded by a quiet, tidy home unlike any she had occupied in North America. The tenements of New York City had been dirty and noisy. They were so unsanitary and unsafe that after Pappa had died, Mamma had refused to live in them. This home was inviting and welcoming, a stark contrast to the Browns' home with polished native wood wainscoting and indoor water closets. There Annika had had the privacy of her own room and a locked door, but even that had failed to keep her safe. She shoved the memory away. Kia's hushed breathing reminded Annika she was with family now. If only she knew these people.

Kia's bed was tucked into the corner between an outside wall and the partition wall to her parents' room, the only private space in the cabin. A fireplace built of large river stones stood at the foot of Kia's bed, flanked on the opposite side with a rocking chair. Annika wondered about the severity of Minnesota winters and assumed that warmth throughout the winter was the primary reason Kia's room opened into the living area. She rolled onto her side, bent her elbow, and propped up her head with her hand. She wanted a better view of the cabin's sparse but reliable handcrafted furnishings she had failed to notice last night. Between the bed and the fireplace, along the outside wall, clothing was suspended on pegs attached to the wall. At the foot of the bed, a long bench spanned the width of the bed. Annika remembered a rag doll lay there next to her carrying case.

Memories of Noak and Kjerstin were dim, and Annika's recall of Sweden was even fainter. She wondered if Kia and Tyko would like her. Did they want to share their parents and home? Sharing a bed with Kia felt natural and drew tender memories of Rebecka.

Across the cabin, in the corner opposite the cook stove, a child, probably Tyko, slept in a bed with one side and the head of the bed affixed directly into the wall. The strange-looking structure extended about a fourth of the width of the cabin. The bed was supported on the front side by thick, smooth posts at each corner that extended from the floor to the ceiling rafters. She wondered how Tyko would feel about having an older child in the family.

Across the full width of the cabin was the loft Noak had mentioned. It was enclosed with smoothly hewn vertical and horizontal posts. A ladder to the loft was incorporated into the built-in bed. Would the loft become her new sleeping quarters? Annika remembered there was a partial enclosed porch across the front two-thirds of the cabin.

Pinkish-orange light stretched across the eastern sky and peeked through the two double-hung windows on the front of the cabin. A spinning wheel sat near the windows at the end of the washbasin. The other windows in the house were small— one next to the built-in bed, one by Kia's bed, and another in her cousin's room.

A table located about five feet from the outside door was flanked on each side by long bench seats with low backs. A straight-backed chair sat at each end. There was enough seating for Annika and a few more. A cast-iron cook stove, which sat a few feet from the outer wall, sprouted an eight-inch-diameter stove pipe that fit snugly into a second chimney. A partial wall a few feet behind the stove created what Annika believed was a small storage room. If there was a window there, it would be possible to look outside in all four directions. Against that wall stood a double-door cabinet that provided storage for the cups and bread Kjerstin had used last night. A large box at the opposite end of the stove, behind the door, held firewood.

Annika crept from bed and removed a dress, another slip, and her hairbrush from her travel case. She removed the slip that concealed her money and donned a fresh slip and dress. She stuffed the other slip into her bag. The dress she wore was snug and gaped between the buttons near the waist, so she rummaged in her bag until she found an apron. She closed the bag and placed it on the floor beneath the bench. She brushed her hair, fashioned a bun, and anchored it with combs. She flipped the apron across a chair back on her way to the door.

Outside, dewy stillness greeted her. There were no early-morning delivery carts rattling down the road to deliver fresh meat, milk, cheese, eggs, and ice door-to-door. Annika leaned against the smooth wooden post that supported the porch roof. Towering trees reached to the horizon as far as Annika could see. Mamma and Pappa would have loved Minnesota. This was what Noak had meant by living "out in the sticks." Beyond the Swedish pole fence, the lake beckoned her to notice a doe and twin fawn getting a drink. Her eye was drawn to a ghostlike figure nearly concealed in the tree line. It looked like a snow-white deer with full white antlers. Within the blink of an eye, the form disappeared. Annika dismissed it as her imagination. She sighed and stepped down onto a well-worn path to the privy.

Annika heard activity inside the cabin and hesitated for only a moment before she lifted the door latch and entered. Kjerstin shut the firebox door and greeted her. Annika poured water into the basin, washed her hands, snatched her apron from the chair back, and secured it around her waist.

"Good morning. How can I help?" Annika asked.

"No, we can't have you working on your first day. Sit and keep me company."

"I must earn my keep. I've done so all my life. I don't want to be beholden," Annika said.

"You've not changed one bit," Kjerstin said with a warm smile.

"What do you mean?"

"When you were a little tyke learning to walk, your parents said you were as independent as a hog on ice. You accepted no help, even when you fell. You simply got up and kept trying." Kjerstin emptied the drinking water bucket into the water reservoir at the end of the stove. She handed Annika the bucket. "Please draw fresh water for coffee. The cistern is by the smokehouse."

"Thank you." Annika took the wooden pail and returned shortly. "That's a little different than having a pump in the house," she said as she poured water into the coffeepot.

Kjerstin added coffee grounds, and soon the aroma of coffee filled the cabin. "I'm sure. You must give me time to learn to share my work. I've done it on my own for a long time." Kjerstin handed Annika a partial loaf of bread and a knife and returned to her work at the stove.

Noak signaled Annika to hush as he slipped behind Kjerstin and hugged her waist.

"Pappa, you're home," Kia squealed. Shoeless, she darted across the floor and into his arms. She hugged his neck and showered him with kisses.

"This is my baby girl," Noak said as he carried Kia over to Annika. The child peeked at Annika and ducked her head against her father's shoulder.

"She's adorable." Annika smiled warmly.

Noak eased Kia into a seat across from Annika and stepped over to rouse Tyko.

"Far, when did you get back?" Tyko asked. He sat up and rubbed sleep from his eyes.

"Your *mor* tells me she really relied upon you while I was

43

away. You did a fine job seeing to things. Come meet your cousin." Noak mussed Tyko's hair and nudged him.

"Can't meet no stranger in my nightshirt," Tyko said.

"Get dressed then." Noak cupped Tyko's head in his hand for a moment and returned to the table.

Annika tended closely to slicing bread. She positioned herself to give Tyko privacy, not wanting to embarrass him. Noak sat down, and Kia scrambled onto his lap. Kjerstin set a cup of coffee in front of him.

"Hello. I'm Tyko." The lad extended a hand.

Annika wiped her hands on her apron and shook hands. The resemblance between the tall, slender youngster and his mother was striking.

"Hello. I'm Annika. I look forward to getting to know you."

"I don't know, you being a girl and all." Tyko grinned, but something in his tone warned Annika it might take a while before he warmed up to her.

"I'm sure you'll give me a chance," Annika said. "Is there anything else I can do?" she asked Kjerstin as Noak and Tyko, who carried the milk bucket, headed to the barn.

"Please help Kia make her bed and get dressed," Kjerstin said.

Annika pulled up the blankets while Kia slipped into her dress and shoes.

"This is my baby." Kia cradled her rag doll in her arms. "She's six months old."

"What a beautiful baby. She looks so much like you. May I hold her?" Annika asked.

"Yes." Kia beamed as she handed the baby to Annika, who rocked her in her arms.

"She wants her mamma. You hold her, and I'll brush and braid your hair. Would you like that?" Annika undid Kia's frayed plait, brushed her hair, and nimbly wove a new braid.

"Where did you learn to braid so fast?"

"My mor taught me. I've been braiding my hair a long time," Annika answered.

"Where is your mor?"

"She got very sick, and she didn't get well. She is in heaven now. That's why I've come here."

"I'm sorry," Kia said, giving Annika an impulsive hug. Kia laid her baby on the bed, and they went back to the table.

"Noak said he invited Oscar for a meal today. So after chores, we'll be cooking—and baking if we can pick fresh blueberries. I fixed oatmeal." Kjerstin set the table with bowls, spoons, and cups.

A clean white cloth and the milk pitcher waited at the end of the table. Noak handed the milk pail to Kjerstin, and the men washed up. Annika draped the cloth into the opening of the ewer and tightly held the outer edge around the circumference of the opening while Kjerstin slowly poured milk through the cloth strainer. Annika filled each cup with milk. Noak offered a prayer, and they shared their first meal.

"What time is Oscar coming?" Kjerstin asked Noak.

"He didn't say. But I expect him bright and early. He was taken by our young friend."

Annika's cheeks burned, and her muscles tightened. Tyko looked confused.

"Don't go teasing Annika before she gets to know us," Kjerstin said. "After we gather eggs, we're going berry picking. Is there any cured meat in the smokehouse?" she asked Noak. Before he could respond, she told Tyko, "Please pick a mess of green beans while we're gone."

Tyko stopped eating long enough to nod consent.

"I'll check," Noak answered. "If it has gone bad, Tyko and I will catch a mess of fish." Tyko followed his father outside to finish chores.

Kjerstin put the food away while Annika filled the dishpan with warm water from the reservoir and washed dishes. Kjerstin put away the last dried bowl just as Kia returned from gathering eggs.

"Kia, put this long-sleeved shirt on so you don't get eaten by mosquitoes," Kjerstin said. She turned to Annika and asked, "Do you have an old long-sleeved blouse to protect you from bugs and poison ivy?"

"I don't have anything. I could put on a different dress," Annika said.

"No, wear this old shirt. That's what I'm going to do," Kjerstin said. "No need for the apron." Kjerstin called over her shoulder as she rummaged on the porch for two woven berry baskets.

Annika donned her shirt, took off her apron, and secured buttons near her waist.

Kia and Annika followed Kjerstin's nimble pace along the winding tree-lined paths. "It isn't safe to venture into the woods alone until you know the area well. This Indian trail was here long before we arrived. It leads to a huge patch of blueberries. Hopefully they haven't all been picked." Kjerstin chatted all the while, maintaining a brisk pace.

"Are there Indians out here?" Annika's tone belied her concern.

"Most left this area years ago. The ones who stayed are no threat."

Annika's mouth gaped open. The bushes hung full with plump, juicy berries. She forced herself to resist popping every third berry into her mouth. The smears around Kia's mouth told Annika the child couldn't resist.

"No more berries, or you'll be sick," Kjerstin told Kia. She grasped the child's chin in her hand. Using her shirttail, Kjerstin wiped the blue stains from Kia's face.

A warm glow touched Annika's heart. The baskets held only a fraction of the ripe berries.

"We'll come back tomorrow after I check to make sure I have enough sugar to make preserves," Kjerstin said.

Annika followed Kjerstin through the woods and wondered at the woman's energy. Kjerstin didn't appear the least tired, despite having awakened at the crack of dawn. Annika was accustomed to hard, demanding work, but she knew frontier life would require great stamina.

"How much farther to the cabin?" Annika asked. "I need a rest if it's much farther."

"I'm sorry. You probably aren't used to distance walking. We'll rest." Kjerstin sat down on a fallen log and motioned for Annika to join her.

Kia scampered about, picking what Kjerstin identified as large-leaved asters. Before long, they were on their way again.

"We're having fish, I guess," Kjerstin said as they stepped back into the clearing a few feet from the cabin.

Annika followed Kjerstin's gaze to three men who stood fishing on the shoreline.

"How many have you got?" Kjerstin hollered.

Tyko pulled a stick from the water and showed off six large fish.

"How are those fish hooked to that stick?" Annika asked.

"That's easy," Kia said. "They pushed the stick through the fish's gill, and that vee at the bottom keeps the fish from sliding off. They keep them in water so they don't die and start stinking before they are cleaned."

"I've got a lot to learn," Annika said.

"We'd better get to cooking," Kjerstin said, taking charge. "Will you prepare these while I mix up the cobbler?" she asked as she handed Annika the bucket of freshly picked green beans. "Kia, you can put your posies in water."

"Then can I go down with Pappa?" Kia asked.

"Yes, after you take off that shirt and wash your hands and face."

The women hung their shirts on the porch. Despite a thorough washing, blueberry juice stained their fingers.

"It will wear off," Kjerstin said as she and Annika set to work.

Annika dumped the cleaned snapped beans into a cast-iron pot and poured the remaining drinking water over them. She went to the cistern, tied the wench rope to the bucket bail, and lowered the bucket into the well until she heard a slosh from below. She unwound the crank another half turn and waited for the bucket to fill. She rewound the crank and hauled the bucket back into view. She maneuvered it to the side, settled it on the retaining wall, and pulled at the tight, wet knot.

"Let me help."

Annika recognized Oscar's rich, deep voice.

His strong, deft fingers untied the knot without effort as Annika stepped back and waited. "I'm sorry if I startled you."

"You didn't. I'm still tired, and I haven't settled in yet. All of this is new, and there is so much I don't know," Annika said as she met his eyes for the first time. She tried to sound more casual than she felt.

"It must be very different. I'll carry," Oscar said, lifting the bucket from the wall. "Noak is building a fire to fry fish at the lake. He didn't want to heat up the cabin unnecessarily."

Annika held the door for Oscar and then busied herself by clearing the cluttered table.

Oscar deposited the water bucket on the washstand and turned to Kjerstin. "I'm supposed to fetch a cutting board and knives so we can clean fish."

Kjerstin gathered the items for him.

"Do you have anything else to put on the fire?" Oscar asked.

"I'll bring the bean pot when I've got them seasoned."

Annika didn't accompany Kjerstin. Instead, she lay down on Kia's bed to rest, until she realized it was the perfect time to snip the threads that concealed the money sewn into her slip. She took her sewing basket and scissors from her trunk, retrieved her slip, and set to work. She estimated that she had approximately $350—perhaps more. Rather than count it, she collected the coins onto a handkerchief and tied up the diagonal corners, enclosing the money securely. She hid the bundle in her trunk. She wasn't ready to explain the cache of money. She stuffed the slip back into her carrying case and lay down again. Within minutes, she was asleep.

◆

Annika sat bolt upright. Her thoughts were jumbled. *That's right—I'm in Minnesota.* That was why she awoke to the aroma of blueberries. She lifted a half-filled dipper from the water bucket and took a long, satisfying sip. She was disgusted with herself. How could she have slept and left the work to everyone else? She walked outside and called to Kjerstin, who was still at the lake.

"Is there anything I can do?" she asked. Against her resolve, she found her eyes straying to Oscar.

"Yes, grab a basket, and meet me in the garden."

"Do you want me to take the cobbler out? It smells done," Annika called back.

"Oh, my dear, I completely forgot." Kjerstin threw her hands in the air and hurried up the rise to the cabin.

Annika watched Kjerstin gingerly slide the golden-brown cobbler from the oven and place it on a trivet to cool. "That looks and smells delicious," Annika said.

"Are you feeling poorly?" Kjerstin asked.

"I'm tired and ashamed of sleeping while others worked." Annika lowered her eyes.

"We've been visiting, and you needed rest. The men are about done cleaning fish. When they finish, we'll dip the fish in egg and cornmeal before they fry them. In the meantime, let's gather and clean some vegetables."

The trip to the garden yielded tomatoes, onions, and radishes.

"Far's heating the skillet, and the green beans are nearly cooked." Tyko handed a heaping pan of cleaned fish to Kjerstin.

"If you'll finish this, Annika, I'll get the fish ready." Kjerstin dried her wet hands and reached for finely ground cornmeal. She turned to Tyko. "Take these, and I'll bring the rest when I'm finished. Tell them we'll eat in the cabin." Kjerstin handed him two large, thick stone platters. "Use these for the cooked fish."

"I don't know what I would have done if I had stayed in New York. I need family now more than ever." Annika sliced tomatoes as she spoke.

"Everyone needs family. That's why we came to North America with your parents. Starting over in a strange country was hard. I wish your family could have continued to Minnesota with us. Things would have been different."

"Mor always told me to tend to what is and don't fret about what could have been. It's good advice but hard to live by," Annika said. "Do you want me to lay the table now?"

"Yes, we'll drink water. I'll be right back," Kjerstin said as she stepped outside.

Annika had the table ready with filled water cups, salt and pepper, and bread and butter by the time Kjerstin and Tyko returned. The cobbler sat on the trivet in the middle of the table. Kjerstin slipped a platter of fish into the oven, and Tyko set the pot of green beans on the stove and left.

"We'll put the food on the stove and serve ourselves. That way, everything can stay warm. I'll put the vegetables on the table."

Annika watched but made no response, because it seemed Kjerstin was talking only to herself.

"That's all of them," Noak said, handing the last platter of fish to Kjerstin. He followed Tyko and Oscar to the basin to wash.

Kia, already washed, waited at the table for Kjerstin to bring her a plate with fish bones removed. Everyone else gathered, and Kjerstin explained the hot food was being offered smorgasbord style.

"Tyko, please return thanks," Noak said.

Tyko cleared his throat and offered a short prayer for the meal and for the safe arrival of his father and Annika.

The men filled their plates. Annika encouraged Kjerstin to follow suit, but she refused. Because she was hungry, Annika didn't dispute with Kjerstin.

"Who caught the most fish?" Kjerstin asked.

"That would be me," Oscar said, "but the real fisherman is Tyko. He caught the biggest. I had to grab his arm to keep that fish from dragging him into the water."

"Did not," Tyko said. He finished his last piece of fish and went to the stove for another.

After the meal, Kjerstin scooped generous servings of blueberry cobbler for the men and smaller portions for the girls and herself. She offered thick, fresh cream from the morning's milk to anyone who wanted it.

"This fine meal is going to make checking fields this afternoon even more difficult," Noak said.

"I agree," Oscar said. "I've got to go to Marine Mills for supplies."

"Would you get me two pounds of sugar?" Kjerstin asked. "Annika and I are going to put up preserves tomorrow."

"Yes. Is there anything you need?" Oscar asked Noak.

"I haven't been home long enough to know," Noak said. "Let's go water Belle and get her harnessed."

Kjerstin gave Oscar money for sugar and began scraping plates.

Oscar lifted his hat from the peg by the door, paused, and then walked back to Annika, who gathered plates and sank them into the dishwater. "It was good to see you again," Oscar told Annika in a low voice as he twirled his hat in his hand. "I hope to see you Sunday." Without waiting for a response, he followed Noak outside.

"What was that all about?" Kjerstin asked.

"I guess he was just being friendly." Annika handed Kjerstin a plate to dry and continued with her washing.

"Let's take a break, and then we'll get you settled." Kjerstin spread the dish towel on the back of a chair and sat down in the rocking chair. "Tyko has been looking forward to moving to the loft. We'll settle you into the built-in."

Annika sat down on the cool stone hearth and leaned back against the fireplace surround.

Kia nestled into her mother's lap and eventually fell asleep. Kjerstin laid her on the bed and motioned to Annika to help move her trunk to the opposite end of the cabin. While Annika fetched her carrying case, Kjerstin rolled Tyko's mattress log-fashion and laid it on the hearth.

"I've made you a new mattress stuffed with cornstalks. We'll have to get started on your winter quilt. I must also finish the feather ticking I'm making for Tyko. This blanket will do until fall."

"I love to sew. I'll help you," Annika said.

"Noak is building chests of drawers for us, but they aren't finished. I hope you can manage with your trunk and these pegs until we can do better." Kjerstin motioned toward the pegs fastened to the foot of the bedstead.

"This will be fine. I'm with family. I've felt so alone since Mor passed," Annika said as she shook out her remaining two dresses and hung them.

"What's for supper?" Noak called out as he and Tyko washed at the basin.

"I guess we'll have leftovers since I waited until the last minute." Kjerstin shoved a small log into the firebox and warmed the remaining fish and green beans. "Noak, would you and Tyko haul his mattress to the loft and get him settled? I cleaned Saturday."

Soon Annika was nestled into her new bed, which rustled softly when she shifted positions. She prayed, thanking God for family and asking for health and strength for the difficult times ahead.

## CHAPTER 5

# NEW BEGINNINGS

Sunday, August 1866

I'm going to church for the first time today.
Being with family makes it easier. Oscar said
he would see me there. I'll try to open my heart
again.

Annika laid the diary and pencil aside. She slipped into work
clothes, went outside, and sat on the porch step. That day,
no deer drank from the lake. Confusion colored her thoughts
with uncertainty. She worried about being among people. She
wanted to see Oscar, even though being near him made her
uncomfortable. She dismissed all thoughts of Oscar because
there was no way he or anyone else could understand. When
she realized Kjerstin was fixing the morning meal, Annika rose
to help.

Annika's heart thumped as they approached the humble
meetinghouse.

"We built this in 1860 because we outgrew the other
building," Kjerstin told Annika.

"It's fifty feet by thirty-six feet," Tyko added, turning
around on the wagon seat.

The sounds of voices and stamping horses' hooves confirmed

folks had already started gathering. The morning air refreshed Annika and helped her collect her resolve. Her plan was to stay close to Kjerstin and Kia, call no attention to herself, and speak when addressed. She nervously redraped her light shawl across her midsection.

Their wagon creaked to a halt. Tyko bounded to the ground and ran toward friends who were peering into a nest on the ground. Moments later, Kia headed in the same direction. Noak helped Kjerstin and Annika from the wagon. Annika smoothed her hair and straightened the gathers of her skirt, hoping to delay entering. Noak and Kjerstin were a short distance ahead, talking with someone she eventually identified as Oscar. He wore the same jacket and pants he had worn the day they met. His hair and mustache were freshly groomed. Oscar's warm smile and long, confident strides toward her caused Annika to feel childlike. She swallowed the dryness in her throat and moistened her lips. She gripped her shawl with one hand and returned a faint smile.

"May I escort you to worship, Miss Annika?" Oscar asked with a mischievous twinkle in his eye.

"By all means." Annika played along but resisted the urge to drop a curtsy.

"Your hair looks like white gold in the sunlight." Oscar leaned to whisper in her ear.

Annika managed a hasty "Thank you" and changed the subject. "Kjerstin said this is the second church for the congregation. What was done with the first building?"

"It's over by Hay Lake, not far from my place. They added a chimney and ceiling to it, and now it's being used as the school," Oscar said. "We moved the church here to be more centrally located because some folks living up north around Prairie Hollow and Bone Lake didn't want to travel all the way to Hay Lake. Except for the size and the large double doors, the two buildings are the same."

"I like the bell tower," Annika said.

"That's a new addition. Noak and I worked on it," Oscar said. They continued in silence, and then Oscar said, "Here comes trouble." Annika didn't miss the edge in his voice. He released her elbow and whispered, "Please wait here."

Annika's eyes followed his gaze. Oscar quickened his pace and blocked Lota about midway between Annika and the church entrance. His broad frame obstructed her view. Once or twice, Lota's hands flailed in the air on either side of Oscar, but Annika couldn't hear a word of their exchange. The longer they talked, the more apprehensive she felt. Eventually, Lota and her companion, an older girl, turned and walked toward the church. Oscar waited a moment and then returned to Annika.

"I'm sorry. Lota is visiting her sister this weekend, and she assumed I would escort her to church. I knew nothing of her visit," Oscar said. He touched Annika's elbow and guided her toward the entrance.

"I don't want hard feelings. Go sit with her if you wish. I understand," Annika said.

"I chose to escort you," he said, and Annika felt her cheeks flush. "Besides, here the men sit together on the right side of the aisle, and the women sit on the left, as we did in Sweden. I don't know why Lota is so upset."

Oscar held the door as Annika stepped into the austere, rustic sanctuary devoid of ornamentation or even a stove to warm the dwelling in cold weather. It felt as if the entire congregation turned and stared as Oscar escorted her to the pew where Kjerstin and Kia waited. *So much for not calling attention*, Annika thought as she sat down beside Kjerstin. Oscar stepped across the aisle and joined the men.

After the benediction, Oscar was again at Annika's side. He stood with her as Noak introduced Pastor P. A. Olander, an approachable middle-aged man with a tidy full dark beard. Annika pretended not to notice Lota's scowl.

"I enjoyed hearing services in Swedish," Annika told Pastor Olander as she shook hands.

"This way, we honor the old country's ways. Were you able to grasp the teaching?"

"My understanding is coming back. In New York, I had to speak English to survive. It's comforting to hear and speak Swedish."

Oscar and Annika followed Noak and Kjerstin toward the wagon, where the children waited.

"Noak invited me for dinner," Oscar said. "I hope you will agree to accompany me on a walk after we eat."

"He did?" Annika's voice revealed her surprise. "Can we invite Kia and Tyko also?" she asked, wanting to avoid being alone with Oscar.

"If you like." Oscar helped Annika to her seat in the bed of the wagon and tipped his hat. He fetched his horse and followed them home.

The children rushed to change into their everyday clothes. Annika exchanged her shawl for an apron, and before long, she and Kjerstin had the meal prepared and the table laid. The family gathered around the table and stood while Noak returned thanks.

"Thanks again for the invitation," Oscar told Noak as he slipped onto the bench beside Annika. "I hope I'm not intruding."

"You're family," Tyko said, and Oscar smiled.

"Family can't intrude," Noak said. "I'm obliged to you for looking in on Kjerstin and the children while I was away."

"Our door is always open," Kjerstin said as she ladled meat and potatoes into each person's bowl.

The warmth of their relationships touched Annika. She longed for the day when this family could feel the same way about her. She would do whatever was necessary to make that a reality. Still, she feared their reaction to the truth. When she'd left New York, she had told herself she would promptly inform Noak of her circumstances—but she couldn't do it. Nor was she able to tell Kjerstin. She decided to wait. She needed time to get to know everyone before she risked disclosing the truth. It was reasonable, but she felt like a liar and a fraud. She certainly wasn't an innocent young girl from New York. She admired and respected these people, and she was reluctant to tell them she was an embarrassment—a disgraced, unwed mother-to-be. Soon enough, they would guess. Her condition became more evident every day. Anyone who had known her previously would have easily noticed fullness in her once slight frame. Her cheeks flushed bright pink with humiliation and anger as she realized, *These people think I'm fat.*

"Annika, are you with us?" Oscar asked as he passed her the bread.

"I was woolgathering." Annika kept talking to cover her embarrassment. "I should be counting my blessings to be here. I'm forever indebted." Tears filled her eyes as she forced a smile.

Kia left her seat, darted around the table, and threw her arms around Annika's neck. "We're glad you are here. Please be happy."

"I am happy," Annika answered as she brushed away a tear that spilled onto her cheek. She kissed the top of Kia's head and thanked her for the hug. Kia, who was obviously proud of herself, returned to her seat.

"Will the Andersens be coming to the schoolhouse cleaning this Friday?" Oscar asked.

"Thank you for reminding me. Will we be doing the soup supper afterward?" Kjerstin asked.

"Yes, but Mr. Peterson, the school board president, wants to have a business meeting before we eat. His wife is fixing a kettle of soup. He told me to spread the word so that other women could bring bread or something sweet."

"We appreciate you keeping us informed of the goings-on at Hay Lake," Noak said.

"It's not nearly a fair trade for yet another wonderful meal," Oscar told Kjerstin, who was helping Annika clear the table.

"Let's clear out and give the women room to work," Noak

said as he pushed back his chair. The men headed toward the cornfield with Tyko and Kia close behind.

"I don't think Lota Robinson was pleased to see Oscar escorting you." Kjerstin dipped water from the stove reservoir into the dishpan.

"I don't know. Oscar spoke to her privately."

"She and her sister were abuzz when they came inside. Lota whispered hurriedly to others before services started."

"I told Oscar it was fine for him to go to her, but he refused."

Kjerstin made no response, but her expression revealed her approval.

"Will we go to the schoolhouse cleaning? If we do, what will you take?" Annika asked. Without waiting for an answer, Annika emptied the water bucket into the stove reservoir and fetched a fresh bucket of water. She and Kjerstin sat at the table and chatted about the coming week's chores until the men returned.

"The corn crop is looking good," Noak said after he stepped into the cabin and dropped his hat onto the peg by the door. Oscar stood in the doorway, twirling his hat in his hand.

"I hope the prices hold up better this year," Kjerstin said.

"If you don't mind, Annika has consented to take an afternoon walk with me," Oscar said after clearing his throat and making eye contact with Noak.

"Who am I to stand in the way of friendship?" Noak said, dismissing Oscar's unnecessary formality.

"Annika requested that the children accompany us."

"I'm tired, Mamma," Kia said. She climbed onto her mother's lap with eyes drooping.

"I'm ready." Tyko dropped the dipper back into the water pail and swiped dribbles from his mouth with the back of his hand. The door banged behind him.

Tyko ran toward the water. "Let's go over to the other side!" he called back over his shoulder to Oscar and Annika, who made no effort to quicken their pace.

"This isn't exactly what I had in mind," Oscar said, "but I'm willing."

"Maybe it will be fun. I've done no exploring since I arrived, and I am curious about the far side," Annika said.

"Tyko, don't get too far ahead, and keep your distance from the shore! We don't want you to fall in!" Oscar yelled. He then turned to Annika. "Are you finding the frontier to your liking?"

"It's wonderful to be with Swedes again. Without family, I've been lonely and without roots. Noak and Kjerstin have been wonderful."

"The loneliness that comes with death is hard to bear." Oscar plucked a leaflike flowered stem and handed it to Annika.

"How pretty," Annika said as she twirled the shaft between her fingers. The stem was topped with a short stalk that sprouted a cluster of individual tiny blue flowers with bright yellow centers.

"My wife, Ellen, called them blue-eyed grass," Oscar said as he plucked a couple more stems. They wound their way around the west side of the lake and across the stream that fed the lake. They followed Tyko's lead.

"May I ask you a personal question?" Oscar asked.

Annika met his eyes for a brief moment before she nodded. She hoped the question wasn't too personal.

"May I ask your age?"

"I'll be fifteen in a couple of months," Annika said as she stifled a sigh of relief. "Why do you ask?"

"I just turned twenty-two. Do you think that makes me an old man?"

Annika felt self-conscious under Oscar's intent gaze. "I'd hardly call you an old man."

Oscar's eyes softened when he heard her response.

"Come look." Tyko bounded back toward them in breathless excitement. "I found deer tracks. One set looks like a huge buck."

"I've seen deer drinking here early in the morning," Annika said.

Oscar went ahead with Tyko. Annika sauntered along behind until a tree stump beckoned to her. She tucked her skirt beneath her and settled onto the warm wood. A rest was just what she needed. She studied the flowers she held. They were the first flowers she had ever received. She shaded her eyes and watched Tyko and Oscar follow the tracks up into the woods. They were in the same spot where she had seen the ghostly white buck watching over his family on her first morning at the Andersens' home. She hoped their exploration wouldn't hamper the deer's return.

"I wonder where Tyko gets his energy," Oscar said. He folded his six-foot frame onto the ground at Annika's feet and leaned back against the stump. They watched Tyko skip pebbles across the water. "I hope we can become friends," Oscar said, peeking upward to look into her eyes.

"I thought we were friends," Annika said.

"Yes, of course, but I mean special friends." Oscar waited for her response.

"I believe someone else already wants you for a special friend." Annika attempted to sidestep his intent.

"Lota and I are only friends, despite what she may tell others. Do you have a special friend?"

"No. I've never received a caller." Annika breathed in short, shallow intervals, and each breath intensified the flutter in her stomach. "The truth is, I'm not comfortable with men since my father died."

"Are you uncomfortable with me?" Oscar's expression reflected concern.

"Not in a bad way," Annika said, "but this is new to me. I'm concerned. You're part of this community, and you must consider what others will think, and so must I."

"So you won't consent to me calling on you?" he asked.

Annika searched Oscar's somber gray eyes and knew he struggled to understand. "I didn't mean that. I guess I'm younger, and maybe I need more time before I begin to court."

"Can we continue our friendship?" Oscar asked.

"I would like that."

Oscar motioned to Tyko that it was time to head back. Annika stood and stretched her back. As they walked along, Oscar plucked more blue-eyed grass and a few blue flag irises.

"How big do you think that buck was?" Tyko asked Oscar as he darted through the field, helping to gather flowers.

"I'd say at least a six-point buck, maybe more."

"What does that mean?" Annika asked.

"It's the number of points on the antlers. The more points on the rack, the older the buck," Tyko said.

"The white buck I saw had a huge set of antlers," Annika said.

"What? There is no such thing as a white deer," Tyko said. "Anybody knows deer are brown with white tails and underbelly."

"I didn't know they existed either. But that's what I saw." Annika refused to concede the fact.

"I've heard tales of ghost deer and bears," Oscar said. "My Ojibwe tribe loggers, on rare occasions, will share an Indian legend. They believe the Creator made plants and animals to live in harmony. He gave each a purpose. According to their legend, the white buck represents the sacredness of all living things. It's a good thing if a person is so fortunate to see one. The men said the white buck causes the onlooker to reflect upon his spiritual life."

A twinge raised goose bumps on Annika's arms as Oscar's words resonated in her thoughts. Was there a reason she had seen that animal in the early-morning mist?

"I won't believe it until I see for myself," Tyko said. He shoved a fistful of flowers toward Oscar before racing back to the cabin.

Oscar tidied the bouquet, added the flowers Annika held, and returned them. He tucked Annika's hand into his and guided her up the rise. He paused at the Swedish fence and leaned against a vertical support post. Annika's gaze followed his across the field and the lake. Grass and flowers bowed in the breeze, and reeds rustled along the water's edge. A fish broke the surface only to plop back into the water.

"This time has been a breath of fresh air for me," Oscar said before he swung the gate open, and they continued on their way.

## CHAPTER 6

# FRONTIER WELCOME

Annika swung the bucket and scrub brush into the wagon bed and laid the handmade broom next to the bucket. She helped Kia into the wagon and climbed in herself. Tyko plopped a tattered blanket into the wagon box, hoisted himself into the wagon seat, and waited for his parents.

"Pappa, can I drive partway?" Tyko asked. "I need the practice."

"Until we get to the main road. I'll take over then. Babe is still feisty, and we may meet other folks," Noak answered.

"I'll sit in back with the girls," Kjerstin said. She handed Annika the food basket filled with fresh-baked bread, eating utensils, and four jars of preserves for Oscar. Noak helped her into the wagon and joined Tyko up front.

"Will there be many there?" Annika asked Kjerstin, who used the blanket for a cushion.

"Last year, there were five families. Tyko looks forward to seeing his friends. This is Kia's first year," Kjerstin said. "I want all my children, even the girls, to get an education. My far made me stay home to help Mor after I learned to read and write. It has been hard for me to learn English—especially the writing part. Do you have schooling, Annika?"

"Cost too much. Mamma taught me Swedish at home. When I started work for the Browns, Mor bargained with Mrs. Brown to school me in English and numbers as part of my pay."

"We want you to attend Hay Lake at least until eighth grade," Kjerstin said.

"I didn't count on that." Annika fell silent. She knew people wouldn't hear of her attending school in her condition. She had to tell her cousins—but now wasn't the time. She leaned back against the side of the wagon and enjoyed the rest and the countryside. She wanted to stay in this beautiful land with her new family but doubted that would be possible.

◆

"Mormor Tille, I didn't expect to see you here. When you weren't at church last Lord's day, I assumed your arthritis was giving you fits." Kjerstin smiled as Noak helped her from the wagon. After he greeted Tille, he excused himself with a tip of his hat, and he and Tyko left.

"Oscar carried me over so I could visit," Tille said.

"This is our cousin Annika, Tomas and Emelie's daughter. Annika, this is Tille Markusson. She and her family sailed with us. Everyone here calls her Mormor Tille, though we aren't related."

"Mor spoke of you and your family." Annika smiled and clasped the gnarled hand that was extended.

"Child, you are the spitting image of your mother as a young'un. Back home, your mor and I were close friends. I hated having to leave the Svenssons back east."

As Annika listened, they gathered the cleaning supplies from the wagon.

The women and Kia passed a small outdoor fire beneath a large cast-iron kettle. Kjerstin paused, lifted the lid, and stirred the potato soup with the ladle that hung from the spit. Annika noticed Tyko and his father at the opposite end of the building with a group of men who pointed toward the roof and the splintered downspout for the water barrel. Oscar captured her eye, tipped his hat, and smiled. Annika's cheeks flushed pink. She acknowledged his bold attention with a cordial nod.

"Nord Amerika has been hard on this one." Tille continued as she watched Kjerstin stir. "My husband passed in the blizzard of 1857—he got caught out in a bad one and froze. After I got the young'uns raised and on their own, I sold the homestead, except for the house. I've got a few extra rooms that I let out to those in need of a place to stay. It's enough to keep me eking along."

Kjerstin hung the ladle, replaced the lid, and set their food basket on the table with the other carry-in food. When she returned, the women continued toward the schoolhouse.

"I guess all have endured hard times," Annika said.

A small group of women had already gathered for the cleaning party. Kjerstin took Annika's hand when they entered and led her into the midst of the group. Everyone greeted one another eagerly.

"This is our cousin Annika Svensson," Kjerstin announced before introducing each woman. "This is Mrs. Olander, our pastor's wife."

The woman impressed Annika as being grave.

"Welcome," Mrs. Olander said. Her warm smile told Annika the woman was reserved rather than grave.

"This is Mrs. Sarah Peterson. Her husband is in charge of school planning."

"It's good to meet you." Mrs. Peterson's manner was brisk and matter-of-fact.

Annika smiled and nodded. As they approached the last woman, Annika realized she had seen her before.

"Finally, this is Molly Jansson. She is the mother of Tyko's friend Ander. She and Lota Robinson are sisters."

"Lota told me about your arrival," Molly said.

"I'm pleased to meet you," Annika said.

Despite the preoccupation with cleaning chores, Annika felt as if she had just returned home after a long absence. Her cheeks grew weary of smiling as she responded to questions and comments. The reception told Annika her cousins were respected members of the community. She longed for such acceptance.

Kjerstin volunteered for window washing and invited Tille to keep her company. Annika and Kia were assigned to dust and wash the furniture using the pail of water and pile of rags provided. The front portion of the room had been swept clean, so Annika started there with the chalkboard and the teacher's table.

"Are you excited about starting school?" Annika asked Kia.

"Yah, but I know little English, mostly Swedish. I write my name and numbers. I will learn more at school."

"I could help you print your name in English. It is only three letters," Annika said.

"Would you?" Kia asked with shining eyes.

The schoolhouse hummed with activity and buzzed with conversation until the work was done, and the men came inside. Mr. Peterson signaled for everyone's attention and thanked them for their help. He reminded parents to tell him by that night the number of children they would have attending school that year. Annika tugged on Noak's shirtsleeve and asked to speak with him.

"Is it very important?" he asked with a puzzled expression.

"Yes, sir, it is." Annika blushed and lowered her eyes. She pushed past his puzzled expression. "I need to talk to you and Kjerstin about school. Maybe we can talk tonight after the children are asleep." Annika wanted to set a definite time so she had to follow through. The guilt she felt about her dishonesty was a burden. These people had been good to her—regardless of the outcome, she had to be forthright. Pappa would have expected nothing less. Annika stepped back with Kjerstin and listened.

"Lota Robinson of Stillwater will assume teaching responsibilities this year. She will take a room at Tille's boardinghouse when classes begin." Mr. Peterson called for any questions or concerns, which were discussed and voted on before the meeting adjourned.

Annika followed Kjerstin outside and watched the women scurry about, unloading food baskets and readying everything for the potluck meal. When Kjerstin had removed her food, Annika took the basket and joined the family. Noak spread their blanket on the ground, dragged a short log from the wood pile, and helped Tille sit down.

"I'll bring your soup and corn bread," Kjerstin told Tille.

Annika handed Kjerstin a second bowl and gave the spoon to Tille. She then delivered bowls and spoons to the others and joined the line waiting for soup. When Annika returned, she discovered Oscar had joined the group. She sat on the ground near Tille and tried to ignore Molly Jansson's eagle eye. She ate her meal and listened to the others.

Tyko and Kia finished first and went off to play while the adults milled about and visited. Annika gathered the eating utensils in the food basket and carried them to the wagon.

"I'm glad you came," Oscar said when he caught up with her. "Are you starting to feel settled in?"

"Yes, although Tyko is keeping his distance. I'm blessed to have family like Noak and Kjerstin." She fretted inwardly about the outcome of that night's meeting.

"No one has a bad thing to say about them," Oscar said. "They are hardworking and always there when a friend or neighbor is in need."

They walked along for some time before he spoke again. "May I call on you next Friday evening?" he asked.

Joy and terror whirled in Annika's thoughts. Why was her life so complicated? She noticed Molly watching them from afar.

"As a friend, I welcome your company," she said, and she changed the subject before he could comment further. "Did Kjerstin tell you she brought you preserves?"

"Yes, they're tucked in my pack. Shall we walk down by Hay Lake, or would you prefer to go back to the group?"

"I'd better go back." Annika turned toward the schoolhouse, and Oscar followed.

Annika dipped her finger into the stove's water reservoir. The water was warm enough, so she prepared a dishpan and washed and dried the dishes from the community supper. The children, tired from their outing, were getting ready for bed while Noak and Kjerstin finished evening chores. Annika put the dishes away, emptied the dishwater beneath the tree in the backyard, and sat down at the table.

She had to tell Noak and Kjerstin about her circumstances, though it was the last thing she wanted to do. If Miss Addie could believe her, she hoped her cousins could also. Back then, Annika's memory had been clear. Now her recall of events was confused. It made no sense. The anger, the trip, and all the changes had stolen her energy. She endured it, and now that she felt safe, she wanted to forget. Annika asked God to give her the words and the strength she needed.

"I saw Oscar walked you to the wagon," Kjerstin said.

"He asked if he could call next Friday evening."

Kjerstin smiled.

"I said he could as a friend. I have never had a beau, and I'm not ready to begin courting," Annika said.

"Oscar is a fine young man. No girl could do better," Kjerstin said.

Noak finished washing at the basin and joined Kjerstin across from Annika. "Did I hear we're expecting company?" he asked.

"Yes, Oscar is coming to call on Annika." As Kjerstin shared the news, Annika blushed.

"Now, what is this about school?" he asked.

"I want to go to school, but I can't. I love it here, but I can't stay. It's not fair to you and the children. Tonight made me realize that." Annika's hands clutched the smooth-hewn wood of the bench seat beneath her. She willed herself to stay seated and finish what she had started. She resisted the urge to flee.

"Have we offended you?" Noak asked, and he and Kjerstin looked to each other in disbelief.

"You've been wonderful. You deserve better than the heartache I bear. That's why I must leave. I shouldn't have come. But I had to get away."

"I don't understand." Kjerstin's eyes searched Annika's face.

"I should have told you before we left New York, Noak. But I was scared." The alarm reflected in their faces frightened Annika and compelled her to continue. "I haven't lied. But I haven't told everything. I'm not sure I can. My memory is empty sometimes."

Noak's brow furrowed.

"When I don't think about it, that's when I feel the best. It was so easy to pretend."

"Is this about your letter saying that you didn't feel safe?" Noak asked.

Annika nodded. She knew it was too late for evasive answers.

"This makes no sense," Kjerstin said. "Take your time, and tell us everything you can."

"I remember writing a letter. I can't remember when I wrote it. I finally talked to Miss Addie because I was so frightened. She made me go to the doctor. He's the one who told me I was pregnant." Annika choked on a sob. The bench she clung to became a piece of driftwood keeping her afloat on a raging sea.

"You're going to have a baby?" Kjerstin said in disbelief. Stunned silence followed.

"This is not right." Noak gave voice to anger. "How could this happen? You are a child. What kind of a man could do such a thing? You must tell us."

The color drained from Annika's face. She felt faint. She couldn't collect her thoughts. Her tongue felt swollen; her mouth was dry. Fear and shame engulfed her.

"I'm angry," Noak sputtered. "You must tell me who is responsible for this immoral act."

"You are frightening her." Kjerstin touched his arm lightly.

"If you want me to go, I understand. I have money. I can rent a room. I'm sorry I've carried this into your lives. I can think of nothing else. I had to get out of New York to a safe place. I'm sorry. This was a mistake." She started to rise.

"I'm not angry with you," Noak told Annika in a calm voice as Kjerstin covered Annika's hand with her own. "I'm angry for you. I know you could never have consented to this. I should apologize; I've lost rein of my temper."

"I know, but there is nothing I can do. Anger poisons everything. That doctor made me so mad." She spoke softly, but she heard the shrill edge in her voice.

"What did he do?" Kjerstin tried to help Annika talk.

"He called me wayward—like I had no Christian upbringing or morals. It wasn't my idea. I got so mad. I walked out, paid the bill, and never looked back. I wasn't going to any children's home. That's where it gets mixed up. Nothing like this has ever happened. My memory is good. I thought I wrote you a letter saying I was coming on my own. I'm not sure. Did you get a letter?"

"There has been no letter," Kjerstin said. "Sometimes letters are lost along the way. Can you remember anything that happened? How can you be sure you are pregnant? Who is the father?"

"I've had no blood flow since before I saw the doctor," Annika whispered. Her face burned. "The doctor said I was due in November. Miss Addie made me go. I get this horrid crushing feeling. It's like I can't bear to remember. It's been so long since I've felt safe. When Noak came, I knew there was hope. I'll make a new life here. Will you help me make a plan? I have enough money to get by until I find a job. Mrs. Brown gave me a letter of reference. I found it when I unpacked." With nothing else to say, Annika lapsed into exhausted silence.

"We are family." Noak took Kjerstin's hand in his and continued. "I'm your godfather, and this is my Christian responsibility. I agree you should not attend school. This is a big problem that is hard to talk about. We need time to consider it. We'll make a plan that is best for all." He turned to Kjerstin.

"The first of the week, you and Annika need to call on Dr. Randall. For now, we will shield the children," Noak said. He pushed back his chair and went outside.

Kjerstin sat down beside Annika and draped an arm around the broken young woman.

Annika collapsed into fretful tears. "I'm so sorry. I've brought shame. I've disgraced my family and ruined everything. I'm going to have a baby, and the father wants nothing to do with me. This kind of thing happens to hateful, brazen wenches, not people like me. It's my fault, and there is no way to make it right."

Kjerstin held Annika and made no response to her intermittent apologies. "You are safe now," she told Annika as she helped her get ready for bed and sat with her until she fell asleep.

The next morning, Annika awoke before everyone else. She lit the candle on her trunk and opened her mother's diary. If only she had kept the diary while in New York, she would have known what happened.

Saturday, August 1866

I am living with my cousins Noak and Kjerstin Andersen near Hay Lake, Minnesota. I'm pregnant and without a husband. I fear I'm losing my mind. I have questions and no answers. I slept better last night than I have in weeks. I finally told Noak and Kjerstin. I want a baby—but not this way. This decision was made by someone else.

Annika closed the diary and blew out the candle. She slipped into her dress and shoes and made her daily early-morning trip to the privy. She paused on the porch and let the serenity of nature comfort her. That day, the doe and her twin fawn drank from the far shore of the lake, reassuring Annika that God ruled all. She whispered a prayer of thanks and asked for strength and guidance. That was when she saw the buck for the second time. She narrowed her eyes and gazed intently into the thicket behind the doe and fawn. Her eyes widened in astonishment. A large white buck with huge white antlers stood guard over his family. She watched until the deer turned away from the water and bounded up the rise toward the buck, and within moments, they disappeared. The sight was real, though it seemed mystical.

Annika returned from the privy, washed her hands, and made her bed. She offered Kia help with the buttons on her dress and then pulled up the blanket on her bed. Annika tied her apron about her waist, went to the cupboard, and got plates and forks. She hesitated to approach Kjerstin, who wore a drawn and strained expression.

"I'm sorry if you didn't sleep well," she told Kjerstin, feeling guilty that she had slept so well.

"Don't fret. I have bad nights every little bit. Didn't you tell me that you really enjoy sewing?" Kjerstin asked.

"Yes, it's relaxing."

"I usually wash on Thursdays or Saturdays, but I just don't want to. I thought we could work on mending and getting the children's clothes ready for school. It will give us time for girl talk. Noak said he and Tyko are going to work in the barn and root cellar, getting ready for harvest. Kia will probably tag along with them."

"I'd like that."

The family gathered for the morning meal. Noak returned thanks for the food and asked a special blessing for the family.

"Would you bring down any shirts or pants that need patching or mending before you leave this morning?" Kjerstin asked Tyko. "And don't forget about socks."

Tyko nodded to his mother and turned his attention to his

far. "After we get the work done, could we swim? Tomorrow's Sunday, and we need baths." Tyko grinned.

"Please, Pappa?" Kia added.

"That might be just what this family needs."

Annika's face flushed hot when she caught the boyish glint in Noak's eyes. Everyone else laughed and eagerly set off to complete the day's chores.

Kjerstin put the last dry plate in the cupboard and started collecting Tyko's and Kia's clothing and her sewing supplies. Annika dumped the dishwater along the potato row in the garden and fetched her own sewing supplies and a few items she needed to mend. They moved the chairs over in front of the double windows. Kjerstin laid the clothing across the seat of the spinning wheel and pulled a low table away from the wall to hold their sewing supplies.

"Kia reminds me of Rebecka," Annika said while she checked the buttons and seams of the child's pale green dress.

"It's hard to lose a sister, a child, or any family," Kjerstin said. She didn't look up from sewing the button on Tyko's shirt, but Annika saw a tear slip down her cheek.

"I think it's especially hard for mothers," Annika said. "Mamma faded a little more with each loss. It started with leaving Sweden and her family behind. It seems like folks collect losses all the way through life."

"True, but we can hold on to the best of life. Here we have land and a way to better ourselves. It wasn't like that in Sweden, where so many needed jobs. During the winter, it seemed as if we were always hungry. Coming here was the right decision for us. We had to do it for our children's future." Kjerstin bit the knotted thread with her teeth to free it from Tyko's button.

"Do you think I could rent a room at Mormor Tille's?" Annika asked. "If I could, then I could start a sewing business. I've always dreamed of that."

"Are you sure you have enough money?" Kjerstin asked. "Most of the women in these parts do their own sewing."

"I have well over a hundred dollars. But I don't know what things cost here. In New York, my daily living expenses were provided." Annika released a sigh.

"I'd worry about you living on your own. We are family, and family is for hard times and good times. A girl your age may need a helping hand at first." Kjerstin's words dangled in the air.

"I just don't want to bring this on your family. Your children are innocent. People can be mean, and I don't want Tyko and Kia hurt because of me. I won't let myself become a burden." Annika wished there was some way to undo the past.

"We'll find a solution. Right now, we need time to consider matters. Then we'll have another talk."

"I tried to talk to my pastor in New York, but it didn't go well. I told him almost nothing before he started offering me money, which I didn't want. After that, everyone at church treated me different and whispered behind my back. I stopped going. I don't want to bring that kind of shame to you. Maybe it's too late." Annika released another sigh. "I just can't think about it anymore." She concentrated on her mending and shut out everything else.

The women worked together until the task was completed.

# CHAPTER 7

# STORMS

Bright August sunlight streamed into the tidy, barren room and accentuated the scent of herbs and medicines that hung in the air. The early-morning wagon ride to Stillwater had been jarring, despite Kjerstin's skilled handling of Babe and Blue. Annika was uneasy in the woods without protection, but Kjerstin had appeared to relish being on her own. Annika shifted in the hard wooden chair, lifted her shoulders, and stretched her stiff lower back muscles. She would handle this doctor's appointment better than she had handled the one in New York City. She was pregnant, and nothing could change that. She was going to be a mother whether she was ready or not. This time, she was determined to act like an adult.

The door to the private office opened and emitted a more intense version of the aroma that already filled the waiting area. Annika looked to Kjerstin.

"Kjerstin Andersen. What a surprise," Dr. Randall said.

"I'm bringing you a new patient." Kjerstin rose from her chair and motioned toward Annika, who remained seated. "This is my cousin Annika Svensson. She is the one in need."

"Come in."

Annika wondered if Dr. Randall noticed Kjerstin's hesitation and her own reluctance. She stood and followed him.

A long table with a pillow at one end occupied one side of the room; nearby a smaller table held a medical bag, a ewer of water and a glass, and a tablet and pencil. Above that table, a shelved wall niche held rows of small containers filled with pills and powders. Strewn with books and papers, a desk was situated in the corner across from the door. Above eye level, three single windows extended across the outer wall.

A framed document hung on the wall by the desk. It looked nothing like the official documents that hung in the doctor's office she'd visited in New York City. This document was simply a business letter addressed "To whom it may concern." Annika paused long enough to read the document, which stated that Dr. Randall had completed medical training under the instruction of a graduate of the University of Heidelberg in Germany, who had begun his medical practice in Washington County, Minnesota, in 1841. When the writer had decided to leave the area, he'd turned the practice over to his pupil, Dr. Charles Randall. The letter was signed by Dr. Christopher Carli. Though he didn't have a diploma, Annika was pleased that Dr. Randall had received some formal medical instruction.

Dr. Randall seated himself after each woman occupied a chair. An awkward silence followed.

"Annika—that name sounds familiar." He turned to his desk and searched about. "Ah, here it is. You came in with Noak about a month ago, when I was gone. Sarah notes that Noak was concerned because you fainted."

"Yes, it was the day I arrived," Annika said.

"Have you fainted again?" Dr. Randall picked up paper and pencil to take notes. "Are you visiting the Andersens?"

"No. I hope to stay here. My mor passed away last year. She was my last remaining family. Kjerstin and Noak are helping me make a new start."

"I'm sorry for your loss," Dr. Randall said, and Annika lowered her eyes. "What is your age?" Dr. Randall resumed his notetaking.

"I'll be fifteen this October."

"Please tell me—why have you come?" Dr. Randall asked.

"I saw a doctor in New York City before I left there. He told me I was going to have a baby. He said I was due in November."

Annika established eye contact. Her cheeks burned. She swallowed hard and continued. "I need medical care for my baby." The voice Annika heard sounded strange—controlled and factual.

Dr. Randall laid aside his pencil and pad. "Can you tell me more?" he asked, avoiding eye contact.

"It's hard to talk about. I won't cry." Annika stared at the sunshine that streamed through the windows and wondered how it could look so wonderfully warm and inviting when she felt so rotten. "A man old enough to be my grandfather broke into my room and attacked me. There was nothing I could do. Now I'm having a baby."

Dr. Randall cupped his long fingers over Annika's folded hands, peeked into her stoic face, and whispered, "I see." Tears cooled her hot cheeks. "Would you be comfortable if Kjerstin stepped out of the office so I can examine you?" he asked as he leaned back in his chair.

"Yes."

Annika followed him to the examination table and sat near one end.

Dr. Randall pressed his fingers along her jawline and neck. He examined her eyes and looked into her throat. Annika declined his request to lie down so he could examine her abdominal area, so he completed the examination the best he could.

"Have you had any pain?"

"No. But I'm always hungry, and I go to the privy all the time. I tire quickly."

"This is to be expected. You should send for me if you experience fainting spells, hard cramping, or bleeding."

"I understand."

"You are small for a woman who is six months along. Your size will increase significantly during the next few months. You should wear loose-fitting clothing that doesn't restrict movement. Given your young age, I advise against lengthy wagon trips after today. You can leave word with Mrs. Markusson if you have reason for concern or need me to come. I'll be in the Hay Lake area in a day or two. I usually travel through twice a month. Do you have any questions?"

"I have nothing but questions. The only one I can think of now is how much I owe you."

"My customary charge is four bits for an office visit."

Annika took that amount from her pocket purse and handed it to him. "I will need to know about the cost of birthing when the time comes. I am responsible for myself and this baby." Annika stood. "Thank you for your time and your kindness." Again, Annika heard the unnatural voice.

Dr. Randall accompanied her to the office door and told Kjerstin, "She is healthy and progressing well. I have advised against long wagon trips after today. If she has a need in the future, I will make a visit."

"Thank you," Kjerstin said.

Annika and Kjerstin stepped outside into a humid, warm breeze and turned toward the general store, where they had tied the team. Before seeing the doctor, Kjerstin had delivered and sold her garden vegetables, butter, and eggs to Mr. Robinson. Now she needed to make purchases. The brisk, short walk to the store eased Annika's nerves.

"I'm glad that's over. I hate talking about it. It is nobody's business, but that won't keep them from talking. This time, I stood up for my innocence," Annika said.

"You are sturdy and determined, with strong, healthy roots like the timber of this land."

"I don't feel sturdy. I do what must be done."

The women paused in the double-door entrance of Stillwater Mercantile. The store was stuffed from floor to ceiling with merchandise. Annika couldn't decide where to begin. She trailed along behind Kjerstin, who requested items the clerk pulled from the shelves and piled on the counter: sugar, flour, salt, coffee, two tablets and pencils, a slate for Kia, and heavy leather for patching shoe soles.

The material and soft goods drew Annika's eyes. She had often run grocery errands for Mrs. Brown in the neighborhood shops, but none of those shops could compare to this. She caressed the cloth shipped from textile mills in the East. Smooth, even cloth with an occasional nubby texture reminded her of Mrs. Brown's fine white Sunday linen tablecloth and napkins. She especially liked the pale green cotton, which she thought would make a beautiful spring dress. She moved down the aisle, touching each piece of cloth as she went—heavyweight blue twill denim for making men's trousers and wonderfully soft flannel. Annika caressed the frothy, baby-soft fabric between the palms of her hands. There was warm yellow and soft blue. She figured in her head. She could purchase a yard of each and hem them for swaddling blankets. If she bought more, she could fashion a baby gown from the remnants. Maybe making a gift for the baby would open her heart. Thinking about sewing soothed her.

"May I help you?"

Annika recognized the wispy voice that sounded as if it uttered each word with more breath than necessary. It had to be Lota.

"Yes, please. I would like a yard and a half of each of these." Annika rested a hand on each bolt of fabric.

"Can't make much from a yard of cloth," Lota said as she took the selections and laid them on the table at the end of the aisle so she could complete her measuring. Annika followed her. "Do we know someone who is expecting a new arrival?" Lota asked, careful to train her eyes on the fabric she cut.

Annika turned her back to Lota and studied the display of thread spools. Should she choose a spool of pale yellow or blue?

"I've invited Oscar to church this Sunday," Lota added. "Mother invited him to dinner afterward. We're spending the entire day together—just like old times."

"That's nice," Annika said without turning around to see Lota greet Kjerstin.

"You found the cloth, I see," Kjerstin said. "I have a spool of white thread at home, and you're welcome to use it." Kjerstin picked up a spool of blue thread that matched the blue cloth she carried. "I'm going to make Kia a dress and Tyko a shirt for school."

"We'll be busy for a while," Annika told Kjerstin.

"Have you gained a bit of weight since you arrived?" Lota asked Annika as she picked up her folded material.

"I hadn't noticed," Annika said, refusing to respond to her snide insinuation.

Kjerstin stood nearby, wearing an expression of scorn and disgust. Annika caught her eye and gave her head a slight wag from side to side. *No need for this to become a nasty confrontation.* That was exactly what Lota wanted, so she could gossip. Annika had seen it all before. She would not sink to that level.

"Thank you for your help," Annika said as she took her purchases in hand and walked toward the front counter to pay. She congratulated herself that her cheeks hadn't betrayed her with an embarrassed flush. Kjerstin followed close behind.

Annika stopped at the peppermint sticks and selected one each for the children. She continued to the front counter, where she paid, and then walked outside to wait while Kjerstin completed her business.

The air felt close and damp, but the sky looked clear. From the boardwalk, she let Babe's velvety nose nuzzle her hand. She was trying to become more at ease with the farm animals. Babe whinnied and tossed her head back, startling Annika, who stumbled backward in surprise. Annika glanced about in embarrassment only to discover Lota standing at the store window, smirking at her. Annika was annoyed, but she held her composure, turned, and walked away.

Annika knew that Lota peered out the window, watching her, as she climbed onto the wagon seat, so she looked directly at Lota, established eye contact, and gave her a friendly little wave. Annika stifled a giggle as she watched Lota flounce away from the window. Annika had hoped they could be friends, but that seemed less and less likely.

Kjerstin's expression changed when she stepped outside, and that worried Annika. Kjerstin hurried to the wagon and stowed her parcels in the storage compartment behind the driver's seat. Annika handed Kjerstin her package.

"I wanted to go to the café for coffee before we started home, but we'd better not with this weather change. I packed food in case we got hungry."

"I thought the air felt different," Annika said. "The sun is shining, but the air seems cool, despite a clear western sky."

Kjerstin maneuvered the horses and wagon north through town and back onto the St. Croix Trail. The stagecoach route was broad and smooth, unlike the narrower trails that led home. Annika took a bread-and-butter sandwich from the food bag and offered it to Kjerstin.

"I can't handle the reins and eat also. You eat, and then you can guide the horses while I have mine," Kjerstin said.

"I wasn't thinking." Annika covered her embarrassment by taking a bite.

"I can talk and drive just fine," Kjerstin said. "I'm so disgusted with Lota Robinson. What she needs is a good spanking. There was no call for the way she was acting. You showed yourself to be the better person, and that's a fact."

"Why give her the satisfaction of getting what she wants?" Annika paused to take another bite of sandwich. "Besides, I've had my share of practice already," she said, hoping to bring the discussion to a close.

They rode in silence for a short distance before Kjerstin spoke again. "I would like to visit with you about your plans. We don't have much chance to talk without little ears." Kjerstin smiled. When Annika made no response, Kjerstin continued. "Have you thought about being alone while trying to support yourself and the child? We wish you would stay with us until we know you will be safe on your own."

"Sometimes I think everything about my life is hard. I don't know what I would have done if I had not found your letter to Mamma."

"Have you considered marrying?"

"I wanted to marry and have a family," Annika said, "but no one will want me. I can't blame them."

"Oscar is smitten."

"He doesn't know the truth."

"Don't count him out without a chance. He has a good heart." Kjerstin paused for a few moments and then continued. "May I ask you how you feel about the baby?"

"I want to love the baby, but I'm so angry."

"Have you thought of letting someone else rear the child as their own?"

"I could never do that." Annika's response was immediate. "This baby is part of me, and he can carry on my family's dream. I will give him my father's name."

"It's a heavy load."

"It must be God's will. Why else would it happen?" She popped the last bite of sandwich into her mouth. "If you'll tell me what to do, I'll try to take over."

Kjerstin reined the horses to a stop. "Take one set of reins in each hand. Hold them firm but not tight. The team knows the way, so you shouldn't have any trouble. If you pull on one rein or the other, the bit in the horse's mouth will turn the horse that direction." Kjerstin handed the reins to Annika and helped her get situated before she reached for the food bag.

"I'm driving a team of horses. Tyko knows they frighten me," Annika said as she guided the horses left onto Ostrum Trail without difficulty.

"New things are strange to a person. He wouldn't feel comfortable in New York City, and neither would I," Kjerstin said as she noshed on her sandwich.

"Was that thunder?" Annika asked.

"I'll take the reins," Kjerstin said. "We'd better push these horses faster. Look at those gray clouds in the north. It's not good when it feels warm and cool at the same time." Kjerstin flicked the reins, and the horses picked up their gait. "I hope we make Marine Trail before the rain starts," she said. "A summer shower won't pose a problem, but we've been known to have tornadoes in August."

Trees blocked the sun, and Annika's efforts to search the sky were futile. The birds were quiet, and no small animals scampered about. The women pushed on, hoping to reach home before serious weather ensued.

"Thank goodness," Kjerstin said as she directed the team right onto Marine Trail.

Wind romped through the trees, and an eerie gloom engulfed the timber. Annika kept her fretful thoughts to herself as Kjerstin urged the horses forward.

Thunder resounded with the force of a massive boulder ripping down a steep mountain glade. The horses lurched forward, and Kjerstin fought to maintain control of the frightened beasts. Wicked lightning flashed. Annika clutched the metal handrail on the wagon seat as she watched Kjerstin tighten her grip on the reins.

"You can do it, Kjerstin. You're doing fine." Annika had no idea what one should do in such a situation, but she had to encourage Kjerstin.

The horses settled into a steady trot. Cool, fitful gusts bantered small twigs and limbs about until calm settled over everything. Kjerstin ruled the reins with a tireless, firm hand and pressed on toward home. Thunder echoed again, and lightning split the northern sky. Rain fell first in sheets and then in torrents. Annika couldn't see beyond the horses' heads. The trees offered protection from the rain but threatened to draw lightning. The situation was grim. Annika fretted about what they could do if a tree fell and blocked the way.

"We need shelter!" Kjerstin yelled. "We should be approaching Oscar's place. Keep a sharp eye."

"There." Annika pointed ahead. A flash of lightning revealed a barn.

Kjerstin drew the team toward the opening just as a man stepped into the tumult and flung the second door flat against the barn wall. The team instinctively sought protection. Kjerstin pulled back hard on the reins. "Whoa! Whoa!" she yelled. The women's drenched clothing clung to them, but they were safely inside. Kjerstin shook.

"I'll bar the door while you catch your breath." Annika eased herself down from the wagon. Her legs wobbled like those of a newborn calf as she made her way to the door just as Oscar dragged the last door shut. Annika held the door while Oscar dropped the crossbar into place.

"Are you wet?" he asked.

Annika's only response was an incomprehensible sputter. The horses stomped nervously, and Annika turned in time to see Kjerstin begin to alight. One moment, she was balanced on the wagon's foot support, and the next, she lay sprawled on the ground, grasping her ankle. Annika and Oscar ran to her.

"What happened? Are you hurt?" Annika asked, falling to her knees beside Kjerstin.

"I've turned my ankle. I'll be fine. Nothing is broken."

Oscar rummaged in the dark and returned to direct the women to a makeshift bed. He helped Kjerstin to her feet and encouraged her to elevate her foot. Annika retrieved an old blanket from inside the wagon's cargo compartment. She sat down beside Kjerstin and wrapped her in the blanket.

"It would be best to wrap your ankle before it starts to swell," Oscar said.

"It may be too late for that," Kjerstin said. "I'd rather not take off my shoe."

"It's your ankle," Oscar said. He found a seat for himself across from the women.

The storm raged outside. They took turns reassuring one another that Noak and the children were safe. Oscar left to tend to the animals. Annika heard him reassuring Babe and Blue as he eased their bridles off and set feed before them. It was incredible how Oscar was always where he was needed. Kjerstin and Annika dozed from exhaustion.

"Kjerstin. Annika."

Annika opened her eyes.

Oscar stepped back and grinned. "The storm has passed. Let's get Kjerstin to the house and put on some coffee."

"I'm fine," Kjerstin said, refusing assistance as she hobbled to the cabin.

Oscar's cabin was orderly and cheerless. Annika helped Kjerstin into one of the chairs that flanked the fireplace and brought a footstool to elevate her foot.

"Are you warm enough?" Annika asked Kjerstin, who nodded.

Kjerstin reached down and loosened the lacing on her shoe. "My foot is still swelling, but I'm more worried about Noak and the children," she said.

"I'm sure they are fine," Annika said as she stepped to the door. Outside, small limbs cluttered the otherwise tidy yard. Annika reckoned it was mid-to-late afternoon.

Oscar filled the coffeepot with water and added coffee grounds. He poked at the coals in the firebox and added two more sticks of wood. "I was planning to have rabbit stew for lunch. Would you like to join me?" he asked.

Annika blushed and looked to Kjerstin, who answered, "Something hot sounds good."

"How may I help?" Annika asked, turning her attention to cooking.

Oscar stepped about the kitchen, collecting cups, bowls, and spoons. He set a bowl of butter on the table and handed Annika a knife and a partial loaf of bread to slice.

When everything was ready, he helped Kjerstin to the table, seated Annika, and offered prayer.

"I'll accompany you ladies home," Oscar said.

"That's not necessary," Kjerstin said.

"I must. That is what neighbors do," Oscar said.

"I'll wash dishes and put things in order," Annika told Oscar.

After the meal, Oscar went to the barn to complete his chores before they left.

"Hand me dishes, and I'll dry," Kjerstin said. She remained seated with her foot resting on a nearby chair.

Annika put away the clean dishes.

"We can make it home on our own. I'd hate to take Oscar away from his work," Kjerstin said.

"True, but he seems determined," Annika answered before she stepped outside and dumped the dishwater. She slid the empty pan onto the shelf beneath the washstand. When she stood, she caught a glimpse of her reflection in the mirror that hung above. She hastily undid her hair, rewound it into a tight bun, and reanchored the combs. "I look a sight," she said as she peeked through the window and watched Oscar load an ax, a rope, and other tools into the back of their wagon. He led Belle from the barn and tied her reins to the back of the wagon. "Are you going to keep the blanket with you?" Annika asked Kjerstin.

"Yes, but I want to ride in the back so I can keep my leg level."

Oscar helped Kjerstin into the wagon bed and onto a pile of dry hay he had added to protect her from the moisture in the wood.

"I'll ride with you," Annika said.

"No, ride with Oscar, and keep him company. I feel drained, and I may nap," Kjerstin said.

Dutifully, Annika climbed into the wagon seat and racked

her brain for something to talk about. By the time Oscar arrived after helping Kjerstin, she was prepared.

"Is this weather common this time of year?" she asked.

"It's not unheard of, but I didn't see it coming."

"We noticed a change in Stillwater and hoped to get home before the storm broke."

"I was finishing my chores in the barn, when I realized it had clouded over. Before I could get to the house, it started raining hard, so I waited it out in the barn. That's how I happened to be there to throw the doors open. That wind would have blown either of you off your feet if you'd had to alight and unlatch the door." Oscar chuckled.

"You can afford to laugh." Annika straightened her weary backbone and lifted her chin defiantly. "I felt like a drowned rat, and that barn door was a welcome sight." She told of Kjerstin's decisive actions and her valiant efforts to urge the team forward despite the rain, thunder, and lightning. "She and my mor are the two bravest women I know."

"Kjerstin is a remarkable woman," Oscar agreed.

They rode along for a short while before he continued. "I find you remarkable. Being stranded deep in the woods during a storm is frightening. Kjerstin told me you were a constant encouragement."

"That was the only thing I could do." Annika shrugged and dismissed the compliment.

"I doubt many city folks would have handled it so well." Oscar wouldn't allow her to discount herself. He craned his neck and looked over his shoulder to Kjerstin. "She's asleep. I bet the ordeal was exhausting."

"Yes." Annika nodded. The farther north they traveled, the more broken and strewn limbs she saw.

"I enjoy your company," Oscar said. "After my wife's death, my life was dark and empty. Each day was a struggle. When Noak introduced you to me, I grasped a tiny ray of light. I look forward to the time we spend together. I hope you do too."

"I value our friendship." Annika wanted to be pleasant, but Oscar's sincerity both endeared him to her and frightened her. There was no way to tell him she couldn't begin a relationship with him without giving him a good reason. She knew it was impossible to bear a child out of wedlock and be accepted by the community. She knew being fully honest with Oscar would make a serious relationship impossible.

Oscar pulled the team to a halt a few feet from the creek bridge. A large tree had fallen, and its limbs blocked the road. He handed Annika the reins and climbed down. He cleared away several small limbs before he returned for the ax. Annika watched him chop a large forked limb in two and pull each piece to the side of the road. With ax in hand, he examined the bridge to ensure it was structurally sound. He grasped Babe's halter and led the team across the bridge.

Annika gasped when the wagon rolled into their clearing. Limbs and branches were strewn everywhere. Relief washed over her as she realized the family appeared unharmed. Kia and Tyko were attempting to gather the hens back into the chicken coop. Noak gathered limbs and threw them onto a growing brush pile. The poles from the picturesque Swedish fence that divided the roadway and the lake were strewn about like matchsticks. The wagon rumbled up the rise toward the house, and the children and Noak rushed to meet them.

Noak helped Kjerstin scramble from the wagon to hug the children and ensure they were unharmed. Noak wrapped her in his arms. "Thank the Lord you and Annika are safe. I was hoping you stayed over in Stillwater."

"I thought we could beat the storm. We got caught in the woods near Oscar's place and waited out the worst of the storm there. He insisted on bringing us home because I was clumsy enough to mangle my ankle. The storm was worse here."

"A twister touched down briefly. We were never in danger, because I had driven the cattle into the barn, and the children and I waited it out safe underground—except for worrying about you." Noak knelt and took her foot onto his thigh. "This ankle is swollen. It may be broken."

"I'll be fine." Kjerstin dismissed his concern, but Noak wasn't convinced.

Annika watched as Noak swept Kjerstin from her feet and carried her to the house. Tyko and Kia followed.

"I'll get our purchases. Hopefully nothing was damaged," Annika said to no one in particular.

"I'll give you a hand and then unhitch the horses," Oscar said. "Noak is going to need help with the roof and the porch repair, and there is no better time than now."

"He's fortunate to have you as a friend," Annika said. She loaded most of the packages into Oscar's arms and carried what remained.

"Neighbors depend on one another out here—especially in hard times. I hope nobody else was hit."

Noak held the door for Annika and Oscar. Annika eyed the cabin for damages and found none. Even the windowpanes were intact.

"I'm going to take care of the horses," Oscar told Noak. "I'll help you get the limbs off your roof before I head home."

"Much obliged," Noak said as he ran his fingers through his hair, reset his hat, and left. The children remained behind to tell Kjerstin about their frightening day.

Annika found the men outside and spoke privately. "I'm concerned about Kjerstin's ankle. Dr. Randall told me he would be out this way in the next day or two. I wonder if he needs to take a look at Kjerstin." She noticed Oscar's mild look of concern, but neither man commented.

"I wanted to wrap her ankle before it started swelling, but she refused," Oscar said.

"Does Doc still stop at your place for coffee?" Noak asked Oscar.

"Most of the time," Oscar answered. "Do you want me to send him your way?"

"Yes, I'll talk to Kjerstin about it later." Noak turned to Annika. "I need your help in keeping Kjerstin off her feet, at least until Doc can take a look. I'd appreciate it if you fixed some supper so we don't send Oscar away hungry."

"I can handle that," Annika said, turning to go while Noak and Oscar discussed how to get the limb off the porch.

"I'll help with supper," Kjerstin said.

"No, please let me. You've had a tough day. I thought I'd stir up some pancakes and make syrup. If any day needs a sweet ending, it's today," Annika said.

"That's the truth," Kjerstin said as she settled back into her rocker. "I hope you realize how attracted Oscar is to you. He has been seeing girls for a while now, but I've never seen him so taken with anyone else—not since Ellen passed."

"If my circumstances were different, I'd be interested. He's been very kind, and he already seems like part of the family." Annika had much more she needed to say, but when she thought about Oscar, she became confused, and words failed her. Annika finally got the fire in the cook stove restarted. She gathered everything she needed to stir up pancakes and syrup and set to work.

"I'll say it again: I hope you don't count Oscar out without giving him a chance," Kjerstin said.

Evening shadows crept across the yard as Annika told Oscar good night. She left the men talking on the porch and went inside to help Kia get ready for bed. Then she cleared the table and washed the dishes, which Kjerstin insisted on drying. Tyko had long since retired to bed as soon as he finished eating. Annika didn't write in her diary that night; instead, she nestled into bed and slept like a log.

## CHAPTER 8

# FIRST DATE

Annika's heart raced, and she clutched the quilt to her. Finally, she realized, *It was a bad dream—only a bad dream.* Even the Minnesota dawn peeking in the front windows didn't reassure her. Would she ever feel safe? Despite being tired from pitching in to help out while Kjerstin's ankle healed, Annika hadn't slept well. The baby kicked, and her hand instinctively went to her protruding belly. She suspected Noak and Kjerstin wanted her to marry Oscar. The thought of marriage frightened her. She hadn't learned how to live with the past, and she was having a baby. She was in no way ready for marriage, even if the baby did need a father. Each time Oscar saw her, his intentions became more evident. However, there was no use in thinking about what she couldn't change.

Annika rose from bed and dressed quickly. She wanted time to write in her journal before the family awoke. She sat cross-legged on her bed with her journal in her lap.

August 1866

> This is a hard land. Noak has been working day and night, getting things back in order after the tornado. I'm trying to keep up with everything. Kjerstin's ankle was a bad sprain, and the doctor told her to stay off her feet until the swelling goes down. Then we should wrap it so she can walk. She isn't happy. She has been sewing

school clothes—school starts next week. I'll
make strawberry shortcake for tonight. I want
to see Oscar, but how do I entertain him? Oh
well. Nothing can come of it.

Annika laid the journal on her trunk and washed up before
knotting her apron around her waist. She couldn't go berry
picking until after the morning meal. She started a fire in
the stove and decided against frying eggs. The hens weren't
producing well since the storm, so she would save the egg for
the shortcake. She prepared a pot of cornmeal mush, flavoring
it with butter and sorghum. While it cooked, she laid the table
and sliced the last loaf of bread. Tomorrow she would have to
bake. She dumped the remaining drinking water into the stove
reservoir and gave the mush a quick stir before heading to the
well. She set the filled bucket back on the washstand just in time
to take the morning milk from Noak. After she strained it into
a large pitcher, she filled five cups.

Kjerstin waited at the table while Noak roused the children.
"Are you sure you can find the berry patch on your own?" she
asked Annika. She ladled mush into each person's bowl as she
spoke.

"I think so. I hope there are plenty."

"If not, I know about another patch," Tyko said. "I love
strawberry shortcake, so we need plenty of berries. Just let me
know if you need more."

"Can I go with you?" Kia asked with pleading eyes.

"That's for your folks to decide," Annika said. She finished
her helping of mush and began clearing the table. She would not
leave until the dishes were done and everything was in order.

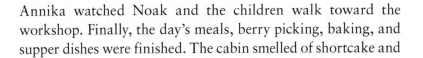

Annika watched Noak and the children walk toward the
workshop. Finally, the day's meals, berry picking, baking, and
supper dishes were finished. The cabin smelled of shortcake and

fresh strawberries. The floor had been thoroughly cleaned, and everything, except Kjerstin's sewing area, was neat and tidy. Annika dropped her apron onto a wall peg behind the stove and went to the washstand to freshen up. The water cooled her pink skin—evidence that a bonnet had not been enough protection for her trek through the woods. She stared at her image in the mirror. Who was this hardy, full-faced young woman with the healthy, glowing complexion? Was she the young woman who owned the strange voice that had spoken so boldly in Dr. Randall's office? Annika pulled the combs from her bun, and her blonde hair cascaded beyond her shoulders. She could wash her hair, but it wouldn't have time to dry. She frowned.

"Brush it out, and wear it loose," Kjerstin said, looking up from her sewing. "It would be very comely."

"No, I couldn't. I'm no trollop!" Annika said, stomping her foot. "I'm sorry. I don't know why I got so angry."

"Child, don't let your circumstances steal your youthful charm." Kjerstin laid her sewing aside and beckoned Annika to bring her brush and sit on the floor in front of her.

It had been ages since anyone else had brushed Annika's hair. The long, gentle brush strokes soothed her. "I can't afford to give a wrong impression."

"Let's meet halfway. I'll pull the sides and top into a loose braid, and only the back hair will be loose," Kjerstin said as she set about her task.

Annika rose to her feet and went to the mirror. She turned to the side and peeked around to glimpse the back of her hair. "It doesn't feel or look like me. Are you sure?"

"You look beautiful. Now, scoot and change your dress before Noak and the children return." Kjerstin folded her sewing and then tucked the notions and the nearly finished garments into her basket.

"Oscar is coming up the road," Kia announced as she bounded through the door ahead of the others.

Annika gasped, inhaled too much air, and started to cough. She rushed for a dipper of water.

"What are you scared of? It's just Oscar. He ain't going to bite you," Tyko said as he shrugged and looked for a place to sit.

"I'm not scared. I was startled," Annika said after she downed a small dipper of water.

"I know it's been a while since we've had evening company," Noak said as he picked up his chair and carried it across the room, "but I think we can handle this."

Annika caught the twinkle in his eyes as he winked at Kjerstin. Annika's cheeks warmed. She fussed with the pleating at the bottom of her bodice. She had altered her mother's favorite blue-and-white print dress to fit herself, hoping the decorative sash would detract attention from her abdomen. She walked to the hearth and sat down to settle her nerves. She appreciated Kjerstin's encouraging smile.

Oscar knocked at the door, and everyone stared until Annika rose and went to greet him.

"Come in," she said with an uneasy air of formality that matched Oscar's dapper attire. He wore freshly laundered dark trousers and a new pale blue shirt that brightened his gray eyes. Obviously, he had taken care to ready himself for the visit. Annika swallowed to moisten her dry mouth.

"I promise not to bite," Oscar said as he stepped inside.

"I already told her that." Tittering accompanied Tyko's message.

"I told you I'm new at this." Annika's cheeks cooled as she gained composure.

Oscar brought his hand from behind his back to reveal a bouquet of small white daisies. "I encountered these along the way and thought you might like them."

"They're beautiful," Annika whispered as the sweetness

rose to her nostrils. "I'll put them in water. Please make yourself at home."

Oscar laid a small carrying case on the table and greeted the others. Annika found a stone container the right height to accommodate the flowers and filled it with water. She listened to the conversation and fussed with the arrangement until she was satisfied.

"Looks like you got most of the tornado damage taken care of," Oscar said.

"Yep, everything but the fencing. I hope to get to that next week," Noak said.

"How's your ankle, Kjerstin?" Oscar asked.

"The swelling has gone down. We'll wrap it in the morning, and I'll give it a try."

Annika set the flowers on the table beside Kjerstin's chair and returned to her seat on the hearth.

Oscar walked over to join her but stopped. "I almost forgot." He looked to Kia and Tyko before he reached into his trouser pocket and pulled out a small, bulging cloth bag. Kia's face brightened, and Tyko waited in anticipation. "If your parents don't mind, I brought along a surprise." Oscar looked to Noak for approval before he continued. "I hope you're not disappointed that it isn't candy."

The children sprang to their feet, and Oscar handed the bag to Tyko. Kia loosened the drawstring, scooped her hand inside, and pulled out three smooth, round marbles.

"Blue, yellow, and red," she said, identifying the colors.

Tyko peeked into the bag. "There is a bunch of them," he said as he looked up at Oscar. "Thank you very much. We'll take really good care of them." He spun around to his mother. "Can we take them outside and play before it gets dark?"

"That's an excellent idea," Kjerstin said. She motioned to Kia to step up and remember her manners.

"Thank you, Mr. Carlsson," Kia said before she shuffled out the door behind Tyko with her fist closed around the marbles.

"If only life were always that simple," Annika said with a trace of a smile.

Before Oscar could sit beside her, Annika sprang to her feet. "Let me get you a more suitable chair. You'll be more comfortable."

"Let's bring the bench over, and we can share it," Oscar said.

Shortly, they were settled on the bench across from the hearth with Noak and Kjerstin on either end.

"Have you been busy?" Noak asked Oscar.

"Yes, I've been getting supplies and crews lined up for work in the pineries. Wish you were going with us this year. I'm going to Stillwater tomorrow to take care of business with Far."

"How far away is the camp?" Annika asked.

"North of Taylors Falls. I'd say it's between twenty and thirty miles from here. It's beautiful country up there."

"How long does the logging camp run?" Annika asked.

"We usually cut into the spring. While the ground is frozen hard, we pour water in the trail ruts, and after it freezes, we pile the timber high on a horse-drawn dray and haul it to the banks of the St. Croix River. When the river thaws, we send the timber downstream to the mills in Stillwater and Minneapolis. It's hard, dangerous work, but I've got a dependable gang of lumberjacks."

Annika searched for something to say. It was too early to serve the shortcake. What was she to do? After what seemed like a never-ending silence, Noak spoke.

"You brought your fiddle. Are you playing again?"

"I don't know if I'd call it playing," Oscar said with a chuckle. "I've been trying to get comfortable with the instrument again. I'm pretty rusty."

"I didn't know you played. My far used to play fiddle," Annika said.

"Please play for us," Kjerstin said. "It's been too long since I've heard fiddling."

Oscar removed the fiddle and bow from the case and sat back down. Annika moved away so he had plenty of room. Memories warmed her heart.

"This was in tune when I left home, but I'd better make sure." Oscar drew the bow across the strings several times and tinkered with the pegs until he was satisfied. "This is the first one my grandfather taught me."

Oscar began with a short, lively tune. He continued with progressively more intricate pieces. Some he identified only by who had taught them to him. Others he played just because he liked them—Annika wondered if any were his own creations.

Noak got up and lit the lantern, and a warm glow enveloped the sitting area.

Oscar played mournful ballads and three-four-time waltzes. Everyone tapped his or her feet with the first and third beat of each measure. They clapped to the beat of the faster polkas and marches.

"It's just my luck to have a bum ankle when I could be kicking up my heels," Kjerstin said. "I never could understand why the church takes such a dim view of fiddle music. It's a wonderful way to relax and remember home."

"I suppose it's like many other things in life: simply a matter of excess," Noak said. The children returned with their marbles and settled on the floor in the midst of the group.

Annika glanced outside. It was well past dusk. Where had the time gone?

"When I get to playing, I lose track of time. Sure don't want to wear out my welcome," Oscar said as he put the fiddle into the case.

"We loved every minute of it," Kjerstin said.

"I think it is time for another treat," Annika said as she rose to go to the kitchen.

"That sounds good," Oscar said. He moved closer to Noak and talked with him in low tones.

Annika wondered what they were discussing. She dismissed

her concern and portioned the shortcake into the bowls she had set out earlier. She set a large bowl of chopped and smashed strawberries on the table along with containers of sugar and whipped cream. Then she filled six cups with water.

"Everything is ready," she said, welcoming them to the table.

Noak and Oscar returned the bench and chair, while Kia and Tyko carefully gathered the marbles into the bag, closed the drawstring, and put the bag on the table by the flowers. Kjerstin hobbled to the table and sat down. Annika ladled strawberries on top of the shortcake. She served Oscar and Noak large portions and was careful to give Tyko extra, remembering how much he liked strawberries. Then she served Kjerstin, Kia, and herself and passed the sugar and whipped cream for anyone who needed more.

"Kjerstin, I believe you have a bit of competition here," Oscar said as he took another bite.

"She did a fine job, didn't she?" Kjerstin said.

"I had a good teacher." Annika wanted to be sure to share credit where credit was due. "And Tyko picked additional berries for us."

They visited about the marbles, the evening activities, and storm damage in other parts of the county. Annika offered seconds, and when everyone was well satisfied, she began clearing.

"It's time for bed for the little ones," Noak said.

"Far, I'm not little. I'm near grown," Tyko said.

"That's right. But mind your manners; tell Oscar good night, and thank him again for the gift."

Tyko and Kia followed their father's instructions and headed to bed.

"Kjerstin and I will take care of dishes if you and Annika would like to take a stroll," Noak told Oscar.

"But that doesn't seem right," Annika said.

"Of course it is." Kjerstin intervened as she took the stack of bowls from her.

Annika shrugged and looked to Oscar.

Oscar held the door for Annika to step outside and then grasped her hand and led the way down the steps. Annika felt uneasy outside alone in the dark, but Oscar's hand offered a feeling of well-being. They followed the lane away from the house and outbuildings west toward the creek. The full moon lit their way, and stars twinkled everywhere. A mild breeze wafted through Annika's hair.

"This has been a wonderful evening. I can't remember how long it has been since I have felt so contented," Oscar said. He stopped, looked down into Annika's upraised eyes, and touched the long tresses that had fallen in front of her right shoulder. "Your hair is beautiful. Please wear it down more often."

"Oh, I couldn't. Kjerstin had to convince me to wear it down tonight." Annika tried to cover her embarrassment by continuing their walk. Oscar's sincerity never failed to confound her and endeared him to her, but fear crept forward.

"I'm going to church with Lota on Sunday."

"She told me."

"When?"

"I saw her the day Kjerstin and I went to Stillwater, and she told me all about her weekend plans."

"I'm going to withdraw from our relationship. It's the right thing to do. I think of you all the time."

"I hope you are sure. There is so much you don't know about me. Please don't be hasty in your actions. Lota cares for you very much." Annika spoke in a hushed tone with strong feeling.

"I know as much as I need to know." Oscar's voice was a husky whisper. His right arm drew her close, and he cradled her chin between the knuckle of his forefinger and his thumb and gazed into her eyes. His expression reflected troubled sadness that Annika herself felt.

Annika fought the urge to pull away. She would not allow herself to hurt Oscar, despite her fear that he was going to kiss her. He drew his hand away from her chin and gently enveloped her in his arms. His sun-scorched cheek brushed hers, and his mustache tickled her ear. Fear, joy, and confusion danced. Annika felt her arms reach around and return his embrace for a wonderful few moments.

Oscar loosened his embrace and searched Annika's eyes. "I will be mindful that this is new to you. Please try to trust."

"You are a gentleman," Annika said as her eyes moistened.

Oscar reached up and swept a tear from her cheek. "I'll walk you back." He stepped back and took her hand in his. "I've got an early day tomorrow, and I'm sure you are tired."

He walked her to the door. Before opening it, he whispered in her ear, "Consider yourself kissed, and I will content myself with that." He winked, opened the door, and bid her good night.

Annika stood in the doorway and watched him mount Belle and ride away. She turned around to find Noak and Kjerstin sitting at the table, apparently waiting for her.

"I know it's late," Kjerstin said, "but we want to talk while the children sleep."

Annika sat down with her emotions in turmoil. She couldn't think, much less make sense of what other people said. She yawned, put the conflicting feelings aside, established eye contact, and listened closely to what they said.

"We are obliged for your hard work since Kjerstin has been laid up. Your parents would be proud." Noak cleared his throat and stared at his hands clasped on the table in front of him. "We are concerned for your future and for your child. We want only the best for you, and we know people can be cruel." When words failed him, Noak looked to Kjerstin.

"We must deal with these circumstances." Kjerstin plunged ahead. "You are far enough along people are realizing your condition. Have you thought of how you will handle it?"

"I thought of sitting at the back of the church alone and leaving promptly after services. I don't want my circumstances to reflect upon your family. If I am not in your midst, maybe they won't shun you. You have no responsibility for my situation, and I want everyone to know that."

"That isn't necessary, but if it is your choice, we will respect it," Kjerstin said. "Of course you are welcome here, but have you thought about long-term things, such as how you will provide for yourself and the baby? How will you raise a child alone? Will you consider marriage?"

"When the baby is old enough, I'll take a job, and I will go out on my own as soon as I can. I already have savings. This baby is my responsibility—there is no one else. I can't think of marriage. No one will want a woman in my circumstances. I must tell Oscar before it's too late. I just don't know how." Annika could feel her energy drain. She lived daily in a deep emotional well.

"I'm thankful you mentioned Oscar," Noak said. "That is what we want to talk about." He looked directly into Annika's eyes for a few moments. "As your godfather, I have obligations to you. I suppose that is why Oscar has come to me. While you worked in the kitchen, he asked permission to call on you. He declared his intention to ask you to marry him." Noak paused.

Annika bowed her head and wept softly. She had no words to express her feelings.

"Oscar is a good man and well respected. He can more than provide for you and the baby when he learns of this." Noak paused again so Annika could respond, but she didn't look up. "I have agreed he can call on you, and I have invited him to dinner next Sunday."

Annika sat with her head bowed, unable to comprehend anything more than Noak's words. She was smack in the midst of exactly what she had sought to avoid. She was angry, but there was nowhere for the anger to go. It wasn't Noak's or Kjerstin's fault. It certainly wasn't Oscar's or the baby's fault.

She was the only one responsible, whether it was fair or not. Anger paralyzed her.

"We love you, and we will stand by you." Kjerstin covered Annika's hand with her own and squeezed.

"I know," Annika whispered.

"We are asking you to consider marrying Oscar." Noak's voice was filled with compassion. "We believe he loves you and that he will accept the child. This is best for you and the baby, and it's best for Oscar. Please give this serious thought."

"I will. Thank you for your concern. I'm exhausted. I must go to bed." Annika excused herself.

Before she climbed into bed, she scribbled, "Now what?" in her journal.

## CHAPTER 9

# A KISS

"Why are you sitting back here alone?" Oscar asked before he stepped across the aisle and sat down.

"I have my reasons," Annika whispered before she returned to singing the opening psalm.

Annika forced her mind back to Reverend Olander's words. What was the matter with her? Why did her mind wander? She needed these words of encouragement and comfort. She had to be strong for herself and her child. She had to make one of the most difficult decisions of her life, and she had to make it soon. She cleared her mind and listened again.

"We know that with Jesus Christ, all things are possible. His love never fails in stormy times," Reverend Olander told the congregation.

Everyone stood and sang the doxology.

"May I escort you home?" Oscar asked as people milled about and visited before leaving for home.

"Oh, I don't know." Annika glanced around and found Noak shaking hands and apparently terminating a conversation with Mr. Peterson. "I'll check with Noak or Kjerstin just to make sure."

Oscar took her elbow and escorted her to Kjerstin and the children.

"Oscar asked me to ride home with him. Will that be an inconvenience?" Annika asked as she stepped close to Kjerstin and spoke in a hushed tone.

"No, no. Go on now. Noak has a couple more people to talk

to before we can leave. Please put the hot rolls and meat into the oven to warm when you get there."

"Can I ride with Oscar? Please, Mamma?" Kia tugged at her mother's skirt.

"Not this time." Noak interceded, leaning in to shake Oscar's hand. "We have to make a stop at the school on the way home. Now, come along." Noak's hand on Kia's shoulder nudged her forward.

Oscar and Annika proceeded to Oscar's open buggy.

"We'll see you both shortly!" Noak called after them before he turned to talk to another member of the congregation.

"This is what you were using the day we met," Annika said as Oscar helped her into the seat.

"Yes, I borrowed it from my far for a few days. It's an easier ride for young ladies. It's been a long week without seeing you. Did you miss me?" Oscar's eyes twinkled as he leaned down to peek into hers.

She redraped her shawl and tried to avoid eye contact, but it was no use. She couldn't resist his disarming humor. "Yes."

"I missed seeing you at church. Last Sunday, I went to Lota's church in Stillwater," Oscar said.

They rode along in silence awhile before he resumed. "I hoped we would have some time alone. I want to talk to you about something."

Annika's moist palms brushed against her shawl as she fussed with the fringed edge.

Oscar continued. "I am no longer seeing Lota, because I wish to call on you only. May I do that? I have spoken to Noak, and he has consented."

"I've never had friends my age or even close to my age. I had hoped Lota and I might be friends, but I don't think she likes me." Annika stumbled over her words. Her thoughts rambled, and her feelings whirled. "I don't know where to turn." Annika released a troubled sigh and stared deep into the timber, wishing she could slip away and disappear. She tried to continue. "I'm not the person you think I am, and there is no way to change that. You deserve more."

Silence swallowed them. Finally, Oscar asked, "Annika, are you afraid of me?"

"No, I admire and trust you. I'm sorry if I've hurt your feelings. You are wonder—" Annika stopped. "I'm not good enough for you."

"Don't you think that is my decision?"

"Maybe, but a person needs all the facts before making such decisions."

"I know enough. We both have shortcomings. We both love God and Sweden. I know you come from a strong, honest family. I believe you are a beautiful, courageous, and hardworking woman who would be a faithful wife. Those are the facts, and that's why I want to court you."

Annika bowed her head as tears washed her cheeks. "I'm so much less."

The buggy rattled over the bridge. "Whoa." Oscar pulled back on Belle's reins. "Now look what I've done. I've made you cry. I'm sorry." Oscar's thumbs stroked away her tears. He lifted her chin and brushed his lips to hers.

Annika resisted the urge to pull away. Her lips curled into a wisp of a smile.

"Maybe I need to do a little less talking and listen better." Oscar's words and eyes questioned her. "I hope you will agree to a short drive this afternoon."

"I'd like that."

Oscar signaled to Belle, and the buggy rolled toward the cabin. Soon he was securing the reins to the hitching post and helping Annika step down.

"Thank you." Annika looked into his pensive gray eyes, and her resolve faltered. She stepped away. "I'd best get those rolls in the oven. The family will be along soon," she said, turning toward the cabin.

"I'm going to draw water for Belle, and then I'll fetch fresh drinking water," Oscar called after her.

Annika felt Oscar's eyes upon her as she walked to the house. Inside, she stirred the embers in the firebox, popped a handful of kindling on top, and added a couple chunks of wood. She watched a small flame gnaw at the wood. Then she washed her hands, tied on her apron, and slipped the rolls and meat dish into the oven before she set the table.

Annika took a small bucket and walked to the garden, where lush red and yellow tomatoes hung from the vines. She set the pail on the ground and used both hands to carefully retrieve tomatoes without breaking the vine. The sun warmed her back, and her mouth watered. She had craved tomatoes all week. A distant clatter of hooves on the bridge told Annika the family was coming. She snatched up her pail and headed to the cabin. She watched Oscar's long legs carry his broad shoulders to the well.

Back inside, she wiped the tomatoes with a damp cloth and sliced them into a shallow bowl. Oscar plunked the water bucket onto the washbasin, and Annika set the tomatoes on the table, near the radishes and onions. Together they filled glasses with cool water.

Annika watched the wagon roll to a stop at the end of the porch. Oscar stepped outside and helped Kjerstin and Kia alight. Tyko bounded from the wagon and headed upstairs to take off his Sunday clothes, and Kia trailed behind. Annika offered her hand and helped Kjerstin, who still favored her sprained ankle, up the porch steps. Oscar swung up into the seat with Noak and rode to the barn to unhitch the horses.

"This looks like a familiar routine," Annika said as Kjerstin washed her hands and took her place at the table. Annika brought her a stool to elevate her foot. "Your ankle is swollen. Do you think you were up on it too long?"

"Maybe, but I've got to start somewhere. I must be fit for the harvest and preserving."

"Hopefully I'll be afoot also. At least this year you will have help," Annika said.

"Looks like you have everything ready," Kjerstin said before turning her attention to the children. "Get washed before the men return. We're nearly ready to eat."

Annika set the warmed platter of side meat at the head of the table and deposited a plate of piping-hot rolls to Kjerstin's charge at the opposite end. She untied her apron and dropped it onto the wall peg behind the stove. She then settled herself beside Kjerstin, thankful for the rest.

"Mamma, why was everyone giving Far money? Do we get to keep it?" Kia asked as she scooted onto the bench across from Annika.

"No. It's money to pay for school supplies," Kjerstin said.

This piqued Annika's interest. She wanted to know more but decided to wait until later. Noak and Oscar had finished washing and were already coming to the table. Noak asked Oscar to return thanks.

"Father God, we gather with thankful hearts and give glory to thee for the blessings of life—for friends, family, and the privilege to serve thee. Please guide us daily in the paths you would have us travel. We ask thy blessing upon this food and the hands that prepared it. Amen."

The group fell quiet while food was passed and portioned onto plates. Annika felt conspicuous as she added a third slice of tomato to her plate, but she couldn't stop herself. She had prepared plenty because she planned to eat plenty.

"How are your collections coming in?" Oscar asked Noak while he buttered his bread.

"I was able to collect from several families before and after services. Everyone is holding to their word, and that is good news. It was good of you to donate firewood last year. Do you expect to do so this year?" Noak asked.

"Yes, schooling is important. One day I will have children in that school, and there is no shortage of wood. I read in the

Stillwater newspaper that the same day we had the storm, there was a vicious windstorm up north that broke off and leveled hundreds of trees. Most of the damage was confined to timber, but part of the St. Croix Trail was blocked. Wells Fargo hired men to reopen the stage route."

"I'm thankful we didn't get hit worse. It was a job to get it cleared. Tyko was busy chopping firewood and splitting kindling most of the week."

"Noak, is it too late to make a contribution to the school fund?" Annika asked.

"I'm always willing to accept money," Noak said.

"I want to contribute five dollars on behalf of my entire family. Mamma had money put away for our trip to Minnesota. I would like to contribute some of that. I'll give it to you this evening."

"Fine."

"Does school start tomorrow?" Kia asked her mother.

"No," Tyko said, "it starts next week, just like I told you."

"She is excited. School is a brand-new adventure for her." Kjerstin patted Kia's hand. "I made an apple cobbler. Is anyone ready for dessert?" Kjerstin asked.

"I couldn't hold another bite," Annika said.

"What if we hold it over for a midafternoon treat before Oscar leaves?" Noak said.

"That's an excellent idea," Kjerstin said. "Since you and Oscar took care of meal preparation, I'll take care of cleanup and dishes," she told Annika.

"It's no trouble. I'll help," Annika said.

"The Andersen family can take care of this," Noak said as he began collecting plates and passing them to Kjerstin to scrape.

"That's a woman's work," Tyko said.

"Yes, but this is America, and sometimes we must change to make our way here," Noak said. "I'm going to help too."

Turning to Oscar, he said, "You two go take your ride. We'll have cobbler when you return."

Annika reluctantly acquiesced and allowed Oscar to tug her toward the door. On the porch, she stopped and gazed south. Sunlight danced on the water, and livestock rested in the shade at the water's edge. A refreshing breeze wafted against her cheeks. She blushed when she realized Oscar was watching her.

"You love this place, don't you?" Oscar asked.

"I feel at home here. It's been so long since I've had a true feeling of home," Annika said. "I'm forever indebted to Noak and Kjerstin."

Oscar escorted her to the buggy and helped her into the seat. He eased Belle back from the hitching post and climbed in beside her. They circled back west past a field with cornstalks dotted with fully formed ears. It wouldn't be long until the corn turned brown and proclaimed harvest. That was good news and meant hard work. The heads of wheat shafts bobbed in the breeze. Annika hoped Kjerstin would be well enough to oversee and direct her in reaping, preserving, and cooking for extra farm hands.

"What are you thinking about?" Oscar asked.

"All the work to be done between now and winter. I don't know how Kjerstin did all this alone."

"Same way everyone does. Put your nose to the grindstone, and get it done. At least for some, there is a break when the wind blows and the snow flies. Noak and I have crops to harvest before I leave for logging camp."

Oscar eased Belle off the main road and up a steep path that wound through timber cleared only enough to accommodate their buggy. Tree branches soared into the air and hovered over the narrow trail, forming a well-shaded burrow through the timber, like an outdoor cathedral.

*Solitude.* "Where are we going?" Annika asked.

"To my favorite place. I happened upon it one day when I was out riding," Oscar said. He pulled the horse to a stop in the middle of the path, sprang from the seat, and secured the reins to a sapling that threatened to encroach on the narrow lane. His hands grasped Annika's waist and helped her down, and she couldn't avoid his penetrating eyes or conceal the desire and confusion they awakened. "We'll walk from here. It isn't far." He reached for the old quilt lying folded on the backseat.

Oscar guided Annika along a path for several feet before he abruptly turned left. He helped her up two large stepping-stones to a plateau in a small clearing overlooking a gurgling spring that disappeared into timber. As far as she could see, there was only the grandeur of creation. Annika's eyes drank in her surroundings. She drifted down to the brook and was greeted by a velvety carpet of wild violets that flowed along the pathway until they reached the bank. The unexpected croak of a bullfrog startled her. Annika searched the bank and finally located the frog sitting on an underwater flat rock with only his head and throat protruding from the water. When a tiny pebble rippled the water nearby, the frog sprang from the rock, plunked into the water, and swam away. Only after she watched the bullfrog disappear downstream did she realize Oscar, who remained on the plateau, had launched the pebble.

He stepped forward and motioned for her to join him. He spread the quilt on the ground, lay down, propped himself up on an elbow, and watched her return.

"This feels like heaven," Annika said. He looked at ease and relaxed, while she felt awkward. Was this proper?

"Sit down, and soak in the beauty," he said.

She accepted Oscar's hand and seated herself a respectable distance from him. Oscar lay on his back, intertwined his fingers, and cradled his head in his palms. The sky was sprinkled with wispy white clouds. Eventually, Annika relaxed.

"My heart is at peace here," Oscar said. "After Ellen's and Hannah's deaths, I was lost. People were good to me—Noak and Kjerstin carried me during those days. But nothing touched my grief or soothed my heart. The emptiness smashed me flat.

I couldn't even feel angry. How could I be angry when I knew they were in heaven? Awaking, getting out of bed, and working meant nothing."

His words echoed Annika's own experiences. Again, she was amazed by his ability and willingness to express himself. She wondered if this ability sprang from his life experience or his maturity. She knew he was more comfortable with himself than she had ever been with herself. She listened with her heart as he continued.

"I took to riding Belle every evening. That's how I happened upon this place—Belle brought me. Finally, I released the loss. God used this place to heal my heart." Oscar rolled onto his side and faced Annika, resting his head on his hand. He waited for Annika to respond.

"Thank you for bringing me here. There is peace in this place." Annika wanted to say more, but she didn't know how.

"I had to bring you here. I hoped it would comfort you."

"Why would you say that?" Annika asked. His comment, so on target, left her feeling irritated and exposed.

"Your melancholy manner reveals that you've encountered your share of heartache. I didn't mean to offend you."

"I'm not offended. I'm afraid of making a mistake—a mistake that can't be fixed." Annika's eyes darted to the brook, back toward the buggy waiting on the path, and up to the serene summer sky. There was no escape.

"We all make mistakes." Oscar sat up and moved closer. He picked up her hand and nestled it in his. "Sometimes they are big ones. The important thing is how we carry on. I want to help. Please tell me why you cried."

Annika lifted her chin determinedly and stared straight ahead. She withdrew her hand. "I'll try. But I don't know if I can." Her thoughts spun as she searched for a sensible place to begin. She remembered the courage she had felt in Dr. Randall's office and the confidence she had felt when she realized she really was the young woman she saw in the mirror the night Oscar came calling. She needed fortitude to proceed.

Oscar waited.

"The other night, Noak and Kjerstin talked to me. They asked me to seriously consider the interest you are showing me. They believe you would make a very good husband for any young woman."

Oscar shifted positions and started to speak but didn't.

"I don't disagree. But it isn't fair to you. I have always wanted to marry and have a family but not this way. You're a man with a farm, a business, and a life of your own. You know what you want. I don't. I'm not prepared for such life commitments. Maybe it would be different if I was older or circumstances were different." Annika stopped and sucked in air. Her throat felt tiny. She doubted that anything she said made sense.

Oscar waited.

"There is no delicate way to say this." She squared her chin, looked into Oscar's sober eyes, and said, "I'm with child." Inside, she collapsed in relief and insecurity.

"I know that," Oscar said matter-of-factly.

"How could you?" Annika asked, feeling hot betrayal. How could Noak and Kjerstin have been so cruel?

"No one told me. Like you said, I have life experience. I knew for sure the night we hugged. A married man learns the difference between a well-fed belly and one heavy with child."

They sat for several minutes before Oscar took Annika's hand again. "Just so you have no doubt, I want you to be my wife when you are ready."

Annika couldn't suppress a fleeting smile. "You don't understand." She maintained eye contact long enough to read the confusion in his eyes. She dropped her chin and said, "I've never been married. That's why I'm not good enough." She couldn't bring herself to meet his eyes.

"How can that be?" Oscar asked. He made no other response for what seemed an eternity.

"It's ugly," Annika answered. "I believe you are sincere, and that's why you have a right to know. If you have doubts, you will realize why I've been so evasive."

"My feelings for you and the child have not changed. The decision to trust must be yours."

"Not talking about it is almost worse than talking." Annika wanted the whole thing over. She recklessly plunged ahead. If she could get the facts out, at least their friendship could be based on honesty. "I don't remember everything. My mind made me forget." She peeked into Oscar's drawn face. "My mor and I worked for a rich older couple and lived in their home just outside New York City. The mistress was kind, and the mister was often gone. He ran her parents' shipping company. It happened a few months after my mother passed. In the middle of the night, he came into my room, clamped his hand over my mouth, and had his way. I couldn't breathe or call for help. I was helpless." Her shoulders shook.

Oscar wrapped an arm around her, and she wilted, numb. "Do Noak and Kjerstin know this?" he asked.

"Yes, as much as I could tell."

"No wonder this has been so hard."

She shifted positions and confronted Oscar's troubled eyes. She had to ease his pain. "You are the first true friend I've had. I'm thankful for our friendship, and I hold you to nothing more. You must be fair to yourself. You're a respected man in this community, and I won't tarnish your reputation. It's bad enough that it has hurt Noak, Kjerstin, and the children. I know I'm the talk of the town. I've carried this alone too long. For today, can we set this aside?"

Annika's eyes returned to the serenity of the brook, and her ears listened to the warbling of the birds. She soaked in the warm sun. Oscar lay back and again cradled his head in his hands and watched the clouds. He may have even dozed.

"What time is it anyway?" he asked as he sat up and stretched. "I bet they are wondering what happened to us. Before we leave, I must assure you that I stand with you regardless of your decision."

Annika wondered how she could have been so blessed.

Oscar stood and pulled Annika to her feet. They folded the quilt and paused for a final look before they grasped hands, and Oscar led the way to the buggy.

## CHAPTER 10

# FENCES

Kia, panting and tearful, slammed through the cabin door and into her mother's arms. Annika had never seen Kia behave in such a manner.

"He's hurt. He's hurt," Kia gasped, and she buried her face in her mother's shoulder and sobbed.

Annika raced outside in search of Tyko. Surely he was the one hurt. She found him trudging toward the cabin. He aimlessly kicked at stones, never raising his eyes. Something was wrong, Annika thought as she rushed toward him. Tyko never acted so lethargic and disinterested. His shirttail hung out of his pants, and his new shirt was torn in two places. He had abrasions on his face and arms, and his nose was swollen, with blood clotted in his nostrils. A black eye punctuated the hostile expression he wore. He yanked his arm away from Annika and turned the full force of his anger toward her. She read contempt in his steely blue eyes. Confusion erupted.

"Don't touch me. I got nothing to say to you."

Tyko's obstinate attitude frightened Annika, but she stepped into his path and persisted. "Tyko, you are hurt. Please let me help. Tell me what has happened."

"You're nothing but a mooch and a liar. That's what he said, and I was stupid enough to stand up for you. Coming home, it started making sense. Everybody in the territory knows. You can't even be honest. You're having a baby, and you don't have a husband. That's why no one talks to you at church. It makes me sick." He pushed past her and headed to the barn, probably to do the chores.

Annika's knees quaked; her strength drained. Would her life ever make sense? She couldn't blame Tyko. It was true. Would it have been easier if they had told the children about the baby? What difference did it make now? She dragged herself toward the cabin.

"He despises me," she told Kjerstin when they met midway.

Kjerstin made no response. With Kia in tow, she turned toward the barn and Tyko.

Annika walked to her corner of the cabin and climbed into bed. She was an outcast. She knew it. She wanted to be left alone.

She slept through supper and awoke early the next morning. She decided to make pudding for breakfast because it was one of Tyko's favorite things. She brewed coffee for the adults and sweetened warm milk for teakettle tea for the children. When everyone had gathered for the meal, she asked Noak for a moment before he returned thanks.

"Tyko, I'm sorry you found out about the baby the way you did. I should have told you. You have shared your home and your parents with me, and I owed you that. I didn't tell your parents until after I got here." She looked first to Kjerstin and then to Noak. "I should have told you before I came. I just couldn't do it. I'm sorry your generosity has ended up hurting your family." She turned back to Tyko and continued. "I didn't know what to say or how to say it, so I did nothing. That was wrong. I failed you, and I failed myself. You are right that I have no husband. Noak is a good, God-fearing man, but not all men in this world are like him. I knew a man who was so mean that I just had to get away."

"Annika's going to have a baby?" Kia interjected excitedly.

"Yes," Kjerstin answered before hushing Kia.

Noak shot his son a stern look.

Tyko stood and walked to Annika. "I'm sorry I was mean

to you. It wasn't your fault Ander slugged me." He stretched a hand toward her as he had the day they first met.

Annika grasped his hand and shook it. "Thank you for defending my honor, even though I don't deserve it."

Tyko, with downcast eyes, returned to his seat.

Noak returned thanks, and they finished a quiet meal. After the children left for school, the adults shared a second cup of coffee with Oscar, who had arrived for a day of fieldwork.

Oscar and Noak worked in the potato field while Annika and Kjerstin pulled the largest garden onions and gathered them in a basket. When it was full, they carried it between them to the wooden enclosure protecting the root cellar entrance. The cool shade was refreshing. They tied the onion tops in clusters of three or four by wrapping long strips of old rags around the stems and knotting them. When that was completed, they took turns standing on a step stool to suspend the bundles in midair by tying the opposite end of the rag around the rafters. The onions would remain there until they were needed that winter. The stretching and bending grew tiresome.

Kjerstin sat in the rocker and rested while Annika took the water bucket to the well to draw fresh water. Frontier life was harder than city life. Here everyone worked from daylight to dark, only to awaken to plenty of work waiting the next day. In New York, she had always been at Mrs. Brown's beck and call, but she had been allowed time to take a break and tend to personal chores. Now she had difficulty finding time to write in her diary. She remembered Sweden and how hard her parents had worked. She'd had precious little time with her father unless she tagged along to work with him. Sometimes she and Isak had helped clear stones from the fields. They'd piled the three-wheeled cart so high that Far had had to rock it to and fro before he could move it to the edge of the field. Once there, they'd stacked the stones atop the rock wall that kept the cow out of the field. Her folks hadn't complained about the work, but they'd hated not being able to get ahead. Once, her mother had told her they seldom knew if there would be enough food for their children—that had made them angry. Hunger was the reason they had come to North America. They'd wanted a better life for their children.

Annika set the water pail on the washstand.

Noak and Kjerstin were proud of the home they had established, and one day Annika would have a home and family of her own, just as her parents had intended.

Annika filled the dipper with cool water and took it to Kjerstin. Then she rubbed her hands with the new bar of lye soap, scrubbed clean, and dried her hands. She refilled the dipper and drank.

"Since we got finished early," Kjerstin said, "let's put together a quick lunch and take it to the field. It'll save the men some time, and we can help pick up potatoes. It's nearly dinnertime, so we'll have to hurry. If you'll pack the lunch, I'll hitch up the oxcart so we can haul potatoes back."

Annika set to work. She sliced bread, slathered each piece with a thick coating of sorghum, and formed several large sandwiches. She settled them in the middle of a clean cloth and tied the diagonal corners into a bundle. She put them in the food basket with the leftover radishes. She wiped whole tomatoes and added them. Then she sliced the last of the cheese, wrapped it in another cloth, and laid it beside four tin cups already in the basket. She filled a large stone jug with water.

Annika carried the basket and the jug to the porch to meet Kjerstin.

"Grab that blanket on the porch." Kjerstin gestured to Annika as she guided the ox toward the cabin. "We'll wrap it around the water jug. Maybe the water will stay half cool until we get to the field. We can spread the blanket in the shade and eat on it."

They loaded the cart and climbed in to ride to the field. The sun dangled high in the sky by the time they arrived.

"We saw you coming, so we kept working," Noak called. "We're ready for a break."

The men selected the dark shade of a sprawling cottonwood near the edge of the field. They dumped water from their morning water jug onto their hands and cleaned away the grime the best they could.

Kjerstin uncovered the water jug and poured each man a cup of water. They drained them.

"Tastes good. Ours has been hot since midmorning," Noak said as both men held their cups out for refills.

Annika turned her back to the men and spread the blanket over the smoothest section of shade she could find. She set the food basket in the middle. She felt uneasy at seeing the men in sweat-soaked shirts that clung to their bodies. Then she realized she must have looked the same. She decided not to be silly. *People sweat when they work.* Bulging burlap bags drew her eyes to the field—every few feet, there was another filled bag. Several feet of ground had been turned up, and golden-tan potatoes glowed in the sun.

"You've been busy," Annika said as she joined the others on the blanket. She took a long drink of water.

"It's a good year for potatoes," Noak said as he bit into a sandwich. "I'm much obliged that you brought us lunch. Now we can have a short rest out of the heat before we get back to work."

"We are going to help," Annika said without looking up. She knew Oscar was watching her, and she felt self-conscious.

She gathered her courage and met his eyes. He winked. She blushed. Why did he do such things? Annika grew suspicious when she caught sight of Kjerstin's whimsical expression. Had she planned this? Annika knew her cousins were concerned about her relationship with Oscar, but they never questioned her. She listened to the others discuss potato yield and market prices. She refilled the men's water cups and tucked the water jug back under the empty corner of the blanket.

"Since you both are being secretive," Kjerstin said, "I am driven to ask. Are there going to be any big announcements in the future?" She looked first to Oscar and then to Annika.

Annika concentrated on rewrapping the cheese. She made no response and waited for Oscar's.

"That's hard to say," Oscar said. "I asked Annika to be my wife. She didn't say no. But she didn't say yes."

"I don't understand." Kjerstin waded into the matter. "Anyone paying attention can see you are taken with each other." Noak sent Kjerstin a cautioning glance, but she continued. "I want you to have the security Noak and I have." She gave a deep sigh and stopped.

Annika knew they had to have this discussion, even through Noak and Kjerstin wouldn't like the outcome. She hated to disappoint them, but she couldn't marry simply for security. It wasn't fair to Oscar or to her.

"It's complicated," Oscar said. "The difference in our ages puts us in different stages. Like she said, I own land, have a job, and have established myself here. She thinks our marriage would damage that. I couldn't care less."

Annika's stomach knotted, her head ached, and her emotions were raw.

"She wants to stand on her own before she makes big decisions. I guess she needs a friend more than a husband." Oscar looked to Annika, and she offered silent affirmation. "I'm disappointed. But with everything she has been through, I must respect her feelings."

"Annika, I only want what is best for you and the baby." Kjerstin glanced to Oscar before continuing. "Oscar can provide protection, security, and so much more."

"Oscar would be a wonderful provider. But if something should happen to him, I'd be in the same spot I was in when I came here." She heard her voice crack as she pushed back tears. "I have to know I can stand on my own and care for my child." She drew a deep breath, and a hiccup escaped, but she forged on. "Everything is hard. I'm having a baby, and I have no idea how to be a mother. How can I be a wife on top of that?" Annika lunged from her seat.

Noak discouraged Kjerstin from following.

Annika stumbled into the timber, and her tears fell unchecked. She sank onto a fallen tree trunk. The others continued debating among themselves, but she didn't care. She needed to be alone.

Never-ending questions whirled in her thoughts. *How can I stop being who I am just to become the person someone else thinks I should be?* The answer, as always, eluded her.

Annika listened to the sounds of the timber. Birds flitted about, and a rabbit dashed across the path, reminding Annika that the world was much grander than her own problems. Gradually, her emotions settled.

Oscar approached, and she hastily dabbed her eyes with her apron. He folded his height in half and crouched on one knee.

"Are you feeling better yet?" he asked.

"I'm getting there. I'm such an impossible baby. They have been nothing but good to me, and I keep giving them heartache." She challenged herself to remain calm.

"They know this is hard for you. It's hard for them too. I don't know how any of us are to make sense of something that never should have occurred. Everyone is frustrated and confused. They need time to consider things from your side. We're going back to work, but you rest for a while." Oscar stood.

"No, I'm going to do my part. There is nothing to be gained by fretting about what can't be changed." She read approval in Oscar's grin and reached her hands out to him for an assist in getting to her feet. They walked back hand in hand.

Kjerstin and Noak dragged burlap bags behind themselves, filling them as they went. Oscar handed Annika her own bag, took his, and headed toward an open row. Annika, with bag in hand, went directly to Kjerstin.

"I hope you aren't too angry with me," Annika said. "I would do anything for you and your family, but I guess I'm afraid to take on more. Please forgive me." She wanted to hug Kjerstin, but she waited for a response.

Kjerstin dropped her potato bag and gathered Annika into a mother's embrace, and Annika felt the tears fall. "I can't say I understand, because I don't," Kjerstin said before she unwound her arms. She looked into Annika's eyes before she continued. "I love you just as if you were my own. I know you would never deliberately hurt anyone. Let us forgive each other and go on from there."

Annika felt her smile spread until her eyes squinted and her cheeks puffed. She hugged Kjerstin with all her might. "Let's pick up taters," she said.

Noak and Oscar looked to each other and shook their heads in bewilderment. Annika impulsively went to Noak and hugged him before she stepped to her own potato row.

## CHAPTER 11

# MENDING FENCES

Annika handed Kia and Tyko each a food pail. She stepped back and watched Kjerstin and Noak stow the water jug and another food basket in the wagon bed. That day, Noak was taking the children to school on his way to Oscar's place to harvest oats. In the early evening, the men of Marine Settlement were to meet at Hay Lake School to decide the harvest schedule. Annika knew that each fall, everyone worked together, sharing time, tools, and equipment, until everyone's fields were gleaned. Noak and Kjerstin had been preoccupied with planning for the past two weeks. Kjerstin already knew the food she would prepare when everyone came to their homestead. She had also planned what she would take to other homes.

Annika was apprehensive about the situation. Her size increased daily, and it took all her courage to attend Sunday church services. She dreaded working closely with others, fearing how they would treat her.

"I've been looking forward to today," Kjerstin said as she linked her arm into Annika's and turned toward the door. "We need some Kjerstin and Annika time." Kjerstin's playful air surprised Annika and made her wary.

Inside, Kjerstin marched to the storage area above the couple's bedroom and settled a small indoor ladder against the divider wall. "Steady this while I climb up," she told Annika, pausing only a moment for her to react. She ascended the ladder quickly and stretched a hand toward what looked like a worn carpetbag. She dragged it toward her. "Look out below. I'm going to drop it." Kjerstin turned her face away to avoid the cloud of dust that arose as she pulled the bag off the edge and let it drop with a thump and a poof of dust only a foot from Annika. Kjerstin descended the ladder and leaned it back against the outside wall before she faced Annika. Annika met Kjerstin's gaze.

"I'm sorry Oscar had to tell me how scary this is for someone your age," Kjerstin said as she grasped the frayed handles of the bag and hauled it to the table. "I should have realized. Now that I do, I want to help."

Annika followed Kjerstin, wondering what the woman was doing.

"I got to thinking that knowing Emelie, she probably passed on most of her baby things after your father's death," Kjerstin said. She struggled to loosen the leather straps on the bag and glanced only briefly at Annika before returning to her task. "So I thought you might need some baby things. I'm happy to make a loan of mine," she said, smiling, as the dry, worn strap gave way.

"I have very few things," Annika said. "I've hemmed the flannel blanket material I bought in Stillwater. I have only those and a couple pairs of knit booties. I've been fretting about getting diapers and about how I will keep them clean and done up." Annika's eyes widened as Kjerstin pulled items from the bag. "These will be valuable during Minnesota winters," she said as she ran her fingers across heavyweight flannel gowns with drawstrings at the bottom. Mamma had long ago explained that the drawstring closure allowed the baby to kick his or her feet and legs without being uncovered. There were a variety of undershirts that tied in front with ribbons, three bonnets of different sizes, and more flour-sack diapers than any one baby could ever have used.

"A mother can never have too many diapers," Kjerstin said. "These aren't fancy, but they are warm. When we get them washed and aired in the sunshine, they'll be good as new."

Kjerstin sorted the items into those that could be washed outside and those that needed to be hand-washed and dried inside.

"This is so generous. Are you sure you want to do this?" Annika asked.

"Of course."

Annika noted a catch in Kjerstin's voice. She was taken aback by Kjerstin's ashen face and now somber mood. Annika hastened to her and embraced the woman as tears fell. She had never thought of Kjerstin as being a person who cried. Annika sat her cousin down and fetched a dipper of water.

"I don't know what came over me. I felt nothing but sorrow. I thought I had accepted the baby's death. Now it feels brand new."

"I'm sorry for your loss," Annika said, covering Kjerstin's sturdy hand with her own.

The women allowed time to pass.

"I hadn't thought once of these things since I packed them away," Kjerstin said. "I never wanted to have another child."

There was silence again.

"Now I'm not so sure." Kjerstin gathered an armful of clothing. "Let's get these things washed, and maybe we'll have time to do the baby bedding before everyone returns. I gathered a few of the children's school clothes to wash when we are finished with baby things." She put the baby items on top of the other clothing waiting in the basket near the door. "Grab the water bucket. That will be warmer than well water, and I'll bring the basket."

Annika did as she was told and followed Kjerstin to the root cellar entry, where the pungent aroma of onion greeted them. Kjerstin set the basket on the ground near a stump and lifted the washtub from its peg inside the shed. She handed Annika the scrub board. She settled the tub on the stump that had been hewn to the right height. Annika situated the scrub board, with its rows of horizontal ridges, in the tub and emptied the bucket of water. Kjerstin directed her to bring another bucket filled from the stove reservoir. Annika returned and found Kjerstin cutting tiny slivers of lye soap into the water.

"We'd better rinse these thoroughly in fresh, clean water before we hang them. We don't want harsh soap to irritate the baby's skin," Kjerstin said.

Annika poured the water into the tub and went to the well to draw more. She refilled the stove reservoir and then set a full water bucket in the sun to warm while the women worked. Kjerstin stepped to the storage shed and retrieved a clean but old, leaky dishpan to hold the clean wash. They took turns dunking and swishing the diapers and baby garments in water before rubbing them across the scrub board. They squeezed the excess water from the clean items and dropped them into the dishpan to await rinsing. Kjerstin dumped her children's garments into the wash water and resumed her scrubbing.

When she finished, the women carried the washtub to the edge of the garden and emptied it along a row of tomatoes. Annika refilled the tub with fresh water, and Kjerstin swished baby items through the water until there was no evidence of soap remaining in them. Annika wrung out the excess water, dropped them back into the dishpan, and began to hang clothes. She secured the items with pieces of whittled tree branches that had been split midway up the shaft. Repeated use had worn the split edges smooth, so they easily secured the clothing to the line.

The clothesline stretched from the door of the root cellar to a large, solidly mounted cross post at the south end of the cabin. The line spanned a grassy patch between the back side of the cabin and the garden. The morning sun had climbed above the cabin peak, and it shone brightly on freshly laundered flour sacks. Annika looked down the line and smiled as she tugged just enough to pull the material taut before she jammed a pin onto the clothesline, anchoring the last diaper to flap in the breeze.

"Don't overtire yourself," Kjerstin called to Annika as she

finished squeezing water from the last items. She dropped them into Annika's pan, and they continued hanging clothes.

"I'm doing fine." Annika shook Kia's dress and hung it on the line by the shoulder seams. "Thank you for lending me these things. I don't know how I will ever repay your kindness."

The women completed their task and emptied the rinse water in the garden. They returned the tub and scrub board to the shed.

"We're family. There is no repaying. We care for one another." Kjerstin scooped up the basket by its handle. "Come on. Let's go inside, and I'll dig out the bedding."

"You are more help than you realize," Annika said as she fell in step beside Kjerstin.

"It's in the chest in my room," Kjerstin said.

Annika turned the opposite direction toward her own small trunk. She raised the lid and removed the swaddling blankets that were nearly finished. She wanted to show Kjerstin her handiwork. She waited at the table, and shortly, Kjerstin returned with a stack of bedding.

"We'll air these quilts. I don't think they will need washed. They were clean when I wrapped them in the sheet and put them in the cedar trunk." Kjerstin laid the items on the table. "What do you have there?" she asked Annika.

"These are the blankets I've been working on. I wanted to show them to you. I hope I haven't misjudged the size." Annika handed the warm yellow one to Kjerstin. "The material I bought was so wide I have enough scraps to make two gowns. I can proceed now that I can use your gowns as a pattern."

"If you intended this for a brand-new baby, I think you have judged the size well," Kjerstin said, and Annika smiled and lowered her eyes. "I thought you volunteered to mend because you knew I'd rather not do it, but your work tells me you truly love to sew."

"I do love to sew. Mrs. Brown taught me how to tat and attach trim to collars and handkerchiefs. Mamma taught me to knit. I want to learn to spin yarn. There is not much call for fancy work out here, but I love doing it. My dream is to have my own seamstress shop someday." She waited anxiously for Kjerstin's response.

"There is no doubt you stitch well enough to do custom work." Kjerstin paused for a moment before continuing. "My concern is whether folks around here could afford such things. Most of us are forced to rely on our own skill."

"That's the problem in a nutshell," Annika said as she began gathering her work. "Somehow, I'm going to find a way to make it happen." She tucked her sewing back into the trunk and returned to Kjerstin. "These quilts are very nice. Were they Kia and Tyko's?" she asked. Without waiting for a response, she continued. "Are you sure you want to loan them?"

"They were, but I'm practical, and we need to make good use of such things. I know you will treat them well. The clothes are probably dry. Let's go bring them in and hang these to air."

Shortly, Annika and Kjerstin returned to the cabin and dropped their armloads of clothes onto the table, sat down, and began folding. Annika started with the tiny undershirts. Before she folded, she checked each seam and ribbon to see if any repairs were needed—those she laid aside. As she folded, she smoothed out the wrinkles. Kjerstin sat across from her, folding diapers.

"Do you want these folded any special way?" Kjerstin asked.

Annika had no idea. She couldn't even remember how Mor had folded Rebecka's. "What do you suggest?" she asked.

"Some folks fold girls' diapers one way and boys' diapers another, and sometimes you just keep trying until you find what works."

"I want a boy so I can name him after my father and brother. Then there will be another Svensson in North America to carry on our family name—as my parents dreamed. Do you think that would shame my family?" Annika asked.

"How could it shame your family if it is done in love?"

"What happened is shameful. Other people don't know the facts, and they don't care. I shouldn't think about it, because it makes me angry," Annika said. "It's hard not to have answers. Why would you lose a baby you loved so much? Why am I having a baby I didn't consent to and am not old enough to provide for? I don't understand. Then I think of Kathleen, so young and without parents, and Oscar and his terrible loss. I don't understand. Does it make sense to you?" Annika picked up a diaper and folded it.

"Death makes us ask big questions, and sometimes everything changes. We may not understand, but God above does. All we can do is trust his will and do our best."

"Oscar wants a chance at happiness, and I want that for him." Annika patted the folds in the diaper before she continued. "How does he have the courage to risk losing again? I couldn't stand to hurt him that way."

"Is that why you won't consider marriage?"

"Mostly, I need to learn how to be a mother. I have to know I can take care of myself and my child if I'm ever completely on my own again. I never again want to feel helpless and without hope. Being alone and having this baby are my biggest fears. I can't imagine being a wife or being intimate with a husband. I don't know. I just don't know."

"I'm beginning to understand. It's just like Oscar said: you need friends and more time," Kjerstin said.

"He's a good friend. You and your family are wonderful. I'm blessed despite my circumstances." Annika gathered the smaller piles together, but she didn't know where to put them. Her trunk had no space.

"Noak, in what little spare time he has, has been working on a chest for you and the baby, but harvest has taken him away from it. For now, let's fold this clean sheet around everything and lay the bundle on the dresser in my room," Kjerstin said. "Oh, I almost forgot. I talked to Kia about exchanging beds with you so you will have more space for the baby."

"I don't want to impose. I've already routed Tyko out of his bed." Annika was reluctant to expect more of the children. "I believe Kia will accept the plan if I give her time to get used to the idea." Kjerstin changed the subject. "We haven't got these delicate little items washed—where has the day gone? It's time for the children to be getting home."

"And we forgot to eat," Annika said with a giggle. "Let's postpone the laundry until tomorrow, take advantage of this beautiful day, and go meet the children."

"Let's do it," Kjerstin said, and they set out on the journey, chatting.

## CHAPTER 12

# HARVEST

The week before, Noak had told them the men had decided to begin corn-husking bees on Saturday at the Andersen homestead and take Sunday off. The first of the following week, they would resume work, making their way north until everyone's corn was picked. He'd told Kjerstin to plan for Oscar and the Peterson, Magnuson, Jansson, Sweedman, and Erickson families. With everyone working, they hoped to finish within the next two weeks. Annika and Kjerstin had spent the entire week planning and preparing. Yesterday, they'd butchered three chickens, fried them, and baked bread and pies.

It was now dawn, and Annika was already tired. She didn't know what to expect, but she was dreading the day. She hoped people would treat her better in the Andersen home than they did at church. She had been receiving a cold shoulder at church ever since she started showing. Many people ignored her, while others whispered and giggled until she came within earshot. It was too painful to confide to Kjerstin, so she suffered in silence.

Annika stood at the door and watched Noak, Oscar, and Tyko roll barrels along the path from the shed to the south end of the porch. The barrels would support wide, rough-hewn boards to form a long table for the food and drink. When the table was finished, the men would set up benches for outside seating. They had long since moved a small table to the east side of the porch, where they added a bucket of water and dipper, a large towel, and a deep wash pan so the men could clean up when they came in from the field.

Annika turned away to help with final preparations. She set up a cleaning station toward the back of the cooking area, near the storage room door. A pan of water, a paring knife, and serving bowls awaited her return. The potatoes, peeled and ready, waited in a pan of water. Kjerstin, who snapped green beans, delighted in the prospect of company. Annika didn't share her enthusiasm.

"I'm going to the garden," Annika told Kjerstin on her way out the door with an empty basket.

The morning sun had risen on the eastern horizon. Annika hoped her trip to the garden would help her avoid greeting guests. She heard the first horses and wagon crossing the bridge. She kept her head down and attended to her work, reminding herself that these folks were coming to help Kjerstin and Noak, not to see her. Annika would be cordial and help with work, but she didn't anticipate visiting.

Annika stepped around the corner of the cabin, carrying her produce-filled basket, and noticed the men were already gathering around the wagons. Earlier, she had overheard Noak tell Kjerstin he would split the group in half and start them at opposite ends of the field, anticipating that each man could pick two rows of corn as the wagon moved down the field. Tyko and Ander held the reins and waited on wagon seats for the signal to move out.

Annika proceeded inside. She smiled and nodded to women who looked up to greet her. She was pleased to see that Tille had come along with the Janssons. She was surprised to see Lota Robinson had also accompanied them. The table was laden with carry-in food and desserts. Annika wondered how they could eat it all. She shrugged and continued to her workstation.

She overheard bits and pieces of conversation but wasn't interested. She tended to cleaning radishes, onions, and tomatoes and tried to muster a better attitude. She dallied as she worked, hoping to make the task last as long as possible. She decided not to slice the tomatoes until closer to meal time. She knew that at some point, she would have to join the group, and she dreaded it. She spread clean dish towels over the tops of the serving bowls and carried the container of peelings down to the hog trough to feed to the pigs. The men had worked their way well into the field. She had heard no one complain about the labor or the heat, and her own poor attitude left her feeling guilty.

Annika went out of her way to greet Kia and Sara Peterson, who played near the wood pile. They had rearranged sticks of wood to form a makeshift playhouse, where they cared for their dolls.

"Do you have company today?" Annika asked Kia.

"Yes, and we have a job too." Kia stood up and pointed southeast between the farm buildings to the cornfield. "When we see the men leaving the field, we are supposed to run fast and tell Mor and the women. It's an important job."

"Yes, it is. I'm sure you'll do a fine job too." Annika smiled before turning toward the cabin.

Inside, she washed her hands and sat down on the hearth near Tille and listened. Time crept along as the women talked of gardening, grumpy men, sewing, preserving, and the quality of that year's wild berries. Finally, Kjerstin excused herself to stir the green beans and potatoes that cooked on the stove. Gradually, most of the women followed her example and began tending to their contributions. Annika and Tille remained seated.

"They surely don't need more cooks," Tille said as she patted Annika's hand. "How are you feeling, child? Are you having any trouble?" she asked.

"I'm tired all the time. Is it possible for me to get any bigger?" she asked.

"It's possible and likely. I myself felt I was the size of a small barn before I delivered my last one. Goodness, that was years ago," she said.

"Tille, when the time comes, will you help with my delivery, even if Dr. Randall is here? I'm so frightened, and I can't take Kjerstin from her family. I'd feel better if you were there."

"Yes, I will. Just send Noak for me. I've delivered my share of babies. The first time is scary, but you are healthy. No need to fret about it."

"I've been getting things ready. Kjerstin is loaning me her baby things. Thank you for speaking to me at church. It feels good to be able to talk about the baby once in a while. If it's a boy, I'm going to name him after Pappa and my brother. Then there will be another Svensson. That makes my family feel closer." Just as she finished, the door banged shut behind Kia and Sara. Annika excused herself and went to slice tomatoes.

"They're coming!" Kia ran to her mother and pulled on her apron to get her attention.

"Thank you both," Kjerstin said.

Annika moved her sliced tomatoes and other vegetables to the table with the other carry-in dishes and walked over to the children. "Would you girls like to watch the men come in from the field or watch the women work?"

"We already watched the men. We want to stay here," Kia said.

"We'd better find an out-of-the-way place for you so you don't get trampled. It's going to get lively in here," Annika said as she reached down and took each girl by the hand. Kjerstin sent her a look of appreciation.

"Can we get on my bed and play there with the dollies?" Kia asked.

"That's an excellent idea." Annika escorted them across the room and situated them out of harm's way.

Annika returned to the cooking area and volunteered to stir the gravy to free Kjerstin to oversee activities. A few minutes later, Kjerstin had everything running smoothly. When the men arrived, Kjerstin spoke briefly with Noak and reported back.

"They want to eat as soon as we have it ready. Until then, they're scooping corn into the crib," Kjerstin said.

"I'll help carry out food and drinks," Lota said.

"Good. Let's start with the breads and vegetables and then the meats and stews. We'll bring the desserts out when the men start washing up," Kjerstin said.

Commotion reigned for the next half hour as the women debated back and forth and completed their work. Eventually, a well-established routine brought calm, until the men started cleaning up, and the hubbub resumed. Finally, everything was ready. Noak asked Oscar to return thanks, and then the eating began. Annika watched from inside. She would wait until everyone had taken their portions, and then she would get hers. Lota had taken her station at one end of the table, where she poured milk or water for each person. She obviously enjoyed the interaction with the men—especially Oscar.

Annika walked away and offered to assist Tille in getting her plate.

"Those steps will tucker me out. Would you bring me a plate?" Tille asked. "Don't fret about what to choose; just put a little bit of everything on it. I always enjoy someone else's cooking."

"I'd be happy to. May I also eat with you?" Annika asked.

Annika found plenty of food remaining. She took two plates and began with potatoes and gravy, green beans, a piece of fried chicken, a small dip of rabbit stew, a piece of ham, and bread. There was no room left for dessert. Lota had abandoned her post of pouring drinks and was sitting with Oscar, chatting while he ate hungrily. Annika delivered Tille's plate and then fetched each of them a glass of water. Annika wondered if this kind woman had come there that day to be a support to her. She hoped so, because the day was going much better than she had expected.

"What would you like for dessert?" Annika asked.

"I love pie and cobbler. If there is gooseberry pie, I'd love a piece and a little spoon of cobbler. I'd better stop at that."

Oscar was getting dessert when Annika arrived at the table.

She waited her turn, until she noticed he was about to take the last piece of gooseberry pie.

"Oscar, would you mind terribly sharing a bit of the gooseberry pie with Tille? It's her favorite."

"Anything for Tille."

Annika searched about for a knife and cut a small portion of the last piece. She put the larger portion on Oscar's plate and the smaller one on Tille's.

"How are you feeling?" Oscar asked Annika, giving her his full attention.

"I have no complaints. I'm looking forward to having this day behind me." She looked up and discovered Lota glaring in her direction. "Thank you for sharing," she told Oscar as she moved on to another dessert. She retrieved two servings of cobbler and went inside.

Annika drank the remainder of her water, scraped their plates, and stacked them by the dishpan before she excused herself to go to the privy.

As she was en route back to the cabin, the shuffling of men's feet and rattling of plates told Annika the gathering was breaking up. She had hoped to be safely inside before that occurred. She didn't want to risk calling attention to herself. She hustled along the path with her eyes downcast. Lota startled her when she stopped her before she stepped out of the shade of the tree growing beside the smokehouse. Lota's face was grim.

"How can you possess the nerve to prance about so shamelessly when everyone is talking about you?" she asked.

Annika, accustomed to Lota's insinuations, refused to be baited into a hateful exchange. She excused herself and stepped around Lota, but Lota blocked her way again. In the confusion that ensured, Lota shoved Annika, causing her to lose her balance and stumble against the tree. Bark scraped Annika's forearm. Enough was enough. Annika drew herself to her full height, centered her weight firmly on her feet, and met Lota's accusatory scowl.

"I don't know why you despise me. I've done nothing to you, and I can do nothing to change the fact that I'm pregnant. I'm trying to get along the best I can. If your only purpose in being here is to deal me grief, please leave, because I have enough grief for two lifetimes." The shrill edge in Annika's voice convinced her she should stop before she said something she regretted.

"Oscar has taken leave of his senses to get involved with you." Now Lota's voice was loud enough to carry beyond their ears.

Annika started to respond but stopped when she saw Oscar step into view.

"You should have stayed in New York, where you belonged." Lota took advantage of Annika's silence.

"Is there a problem?" Oscar asked as he stepped toward them, and Annika watched Lota's flushed face go ashen before she spun around and confronted him.

"Everything is just fine," Lota sputtered as she stalked away.

"What's this about?" Oscar asked Annika.

"It doesn't matter," Annika said before she followed in Lota's footsteps, shutting out the peering eyes she encountered. Annika searched the eating area without locating Kjerstin. She couldn't miss Lota gesturing wildly as she talked with her sister, but Annika wanted only to escape inside.

When she located Kjerstin, she said, "I'm not feeling well, and I need some privacy. May I rest in your room?"

"Of course. Are you ill?"

"No, I just need to rest." Annika glanced outside as she passed the doorway. Oscar had joined Lota and Molly. Too emotionally drained to care, Annika made her way to Kjerstin's room. A refreshing, mild breeze entered through the open south window. She felt better the moment she was off her swollen feet.

The clattering of dishes, pots, and pans subsided once the women returned the food to the kitchen. Annika knew they were busy scraping, washing, and drying dishes.

She closed her eyes and drifted into comfort, until she heard Oscar's voice. Her eyes popped open. Maybe she had imagined the sound. She listened. Yes, it was his voice outside the window. She felt small-minded and mean for eavesdropping, but she had to know what was happening.

"Let go of me. You're hurting me," said a voice Annika recognized as Lota's.

"I'm not hurting you. I only escorted you to a private place to talk," Oscar said. "If you're angry with me, you should talk to me. This has nothing to do with Annika."

"None of this would have happened if she had stayed in New York," Lota said.

"That has no bearing on this."

Annika heard the patience in Oscar's voice as he reasoned with Lota.

"We have always been friends. I've never promised more. I spoke to your father about nothing more than courting. I'm sorry if you are hurt because I'm no longer calling on you."

"You're just saying that. We got along fine before she arrived."

"We were friends. I would like to think we are still friends. The truth is, Annika has discouraged my intentions. She cautioned me about being too hasty in not calling on you. I see no more than friendship in our future, and that's why I decided it was unfair to you to continue calling on you."

"You can't deny you are smitten with her," Lota said, and Annika held her breath.

"No, I can't, but I have no idea how that will proceed. My concern now is that Annika has enough to endure without being publicly humiliated. Please leave her alone."

A tear slipped from the corner of Annika's eye. She didn't want to keep listening, but she did.

"I have no obligation to you," Lota said. "Now, if you'll excuse me, I've been asked to leave, and I must talk to Molly."

"And I need to get to work," Oscar said.

"Molly!" Lota called to her sister. "Where is Olle?"

"He's not coming," Molly's fainter voice answered. Molly joined Lota beneath the window. "We must have help in harvesting our corn, so he is staying to finish the job. We'll walk back to Tille's place and wait there until he and Ander come for us. I'll tell the women we are leaving."

The screen door closed for the second time as Annika slipped to the window and watched Lota and Molly walk down the sloping lane along the Swedish fence Noak had repaired. She wondered why life was so complicated. She returned to bed for a short nap, but sleep eluded her. Oscar's statement that he didn't know how things would proceed for them echoed in her thoughts. Was he having second thoughts? Had he changed his mind? Sleep came before an answer.

Annika judged it to be late afternoon when she awoke. She had to rejoin the women, whether she wanted to or not. She figured she might as well face them now rather than wait until she arrived at church tomorrow. She didn't care what they thought about her, but she did care what Tille, Kjerstin, and Noak thought. She would not disappoint them by being mean-spirited; besides, the nap had been refreshing. She tucked stray hairs back into her bun and opened the door.

"We were just fixing tea. Would you like a cup?" Kjerstin asked Annika, looking up from her work at the stove. None of the other women acknowledged Annika.

"I'll just have water," Annika said as she lifted the dipper to her mouth. When she finished, she sat down at the table next to Tille. "How much longer do you suppose the work will go on?" Annika asked the older woman.

"From what I've heard, they expect to be finished before nightfall. That's why the women are warming leftovers. There were still enough victuals for a small army. I expect the supper dishes will be left to you and Kjerstin. Are you feeling up to that?" she asked.

"Yes, I'm fine. I got overly tired and ran out of patience," Annika said, avoiding Tille's unspoken question.

◆

Annika bid Tille a warm farewell and accompanied her to the porch, where Kjerstin helped Tille down the steps and over to Olle's wagon. The other women were clustered nearby, visiting. Annika promptly went back inside and began scraping dishes. She dipped water from the stove into the dishpan. She washed dishes until she ran out of draining room. Then she stopped to dry them and put them away. She continued the routine and had nearly finished by the time Kjerstin and Noak sent the children inside to bed before bidding Olle and Tille goodbye.

Annika was speechless when she looked up and found Oscar standing in the doorway, twirling his hat in his hand as if debating what to do next. His smile brightened her mood.

"Could I interest you in something to drink?" she asked.

"Just a glass of water, please," he said, stepping toward her. "May I talk with you for a few minutes?"

Annika wondered why he was so ill at ease. Regardless, she motioned for him to take a seat at the table and delivered his water. She sat down across from him.

"I must apologize for Lota's poor manners, because I don't believe she will do so. She had no right to talk to you as she did," Oscar said.

"She has been hurt by my coming here. I can understand that." Annika wasn't sure what else to say, but she continued. "She is responsible, not you. Besides, I'm not proud of myself either. It wasn't my place to ask her to leave." Annika wouldn't tell him about the overheard conversation.

"I'm thankful you did," Oscar said with a slight grin. "Our friendship is important to me."

Annika's heart soared.

"And I hope complications with Lota won't change that," Oscar added as he rose to leave.

Annika stood and tentatively touched his arm. "Thank you for caring about my feelings." She drew back her hand when Kjerstin and Noak entered.

"If tomorrow wasn't Sunday and this hadn't been such a long day, I'd invite you to stay and visit," Noak said as he clapped Oscar on the back. "Thank you for all your help today."

"Anytime, neighbor," Oscar said as he tipped his hat to Annika and headed back outside with Noak.

Annika sank back onto the bench, thankful the day had finally ended.

"What happened with Lota?" Kjerstin asked as she put away the last of the dishes.

"She's angry with me because Oscar stopped calling on her. I don't blame her, even if it's not my fault." Annika wanted the conversation to end there, but she knew she owed Kjerstin and Noak an apology. "I think she shoved me, and I got so frustrated I asked her to leave. That was unkind, and it was not my place. I'm sorry for offending your guest."

"This is your home too, and most people defend themselves when threatened," Kjerstin said. "Is that why you needed to lie down, or were you ill?"

"I was tired, but it was mostly the run-in with Lota. I felt much better after my nap."

"Why don't you turn in? It's been a long day for all of us," Kjerstin said as she briefly embraced Annika.

## CHAPTER 13

# BIRTH

Annika sat at the table and leafed through her journal. An entry dated a few weeks earlier caught her eye.

Thursday, October 1866

> Reverend and Mrs. Olander just left. I'm not sure if they came to see me or Noak and Kjerstin, who are working with the harvest crews. I stayed home so someone would be here when school was out. They are trying to protect the outcast. Reverend Olander tried to help me understand why these things have happened. He says forgiveness is the only way. I'm not sure what that means, but I promised to think about it. He offered to come back to study with me again, and I agreed.

Annika skipped forward to a more recent entry.

Tuesday, November 1866

> Oscar stayed for supper tonight. He leaves for the pineries tomorrow morning. I don't know how I'm going to make it through the winter. I miss him already.

Annika sighed, closed the diary, and laid it aside. She was beginning to realize the importance of Oscar's friendship. The prospect of winter was bleak, and spring was too far away.

"Feeling lonesome?" Kjerstin asked as she looked up from the dough she had been kneading.

"Yes," Annika answered as she watched Kjerstin skillfully form loaves, slip them into buttery baking tins, and cover them with a clean cloth before she moved on to shaping buns for the evening meal. Annika wanted to help, but her back ached. Every inch of her body felt swollen, as if she would burst. She went to the stove and poked at the red-hot coals in the firebox. She added two more sticks of wood. Fire warmed the brisk November morning. Annika knew the aroma of baking bread would sweeten her mood.

A sharp pain shot through her lower back as she turned from the stove to sit down. She willed herself to relax before the pain could intensify. She eased herself into a chair.

"What if I can't do it?" she asked Kjerstin as she watched her slide the bread into the oven. "What if I'm a screamer?"

"You wouldn't be the first or the last. Birthing babies has been going on since the Garden of Eden. It's as natural as day and night," Kjerstin said as she turned her attention to tidying up. "Are you having hard pains?"

"Maybe. I had a couple pains just before dawn but nothing until now." Annika shifted positions under Kjerstin's vigilant gaze.

"I'm going to prepare your bed." Kjerstin scurried toward the back of the cabin, where Annika now slept since she and Kia had exchanged beds. "We'll need plenty of bedding and protective padding when the time comes." Kjerstin chattered as she worked. "Maybe lying down and stretching out would feel good."

Annika accepted Kjerstin's arm for support. She hesitated for a moment and then gave a sigh of relief because there was no pain. They crossed the floor, and Annika eased onto the edge of the bed. Kjerstin lifted Annika's swollen feet onto the bed.

"Aah, this does feel good." Annika smiled into Kjerstin's concerned face. "I'm fine," Annika told her. The truth was, her feet ached, and being off them felt wonderful.

"Doc left word that he would be gone on calls to Taylors Falls this week." Kjerstin fretted.

"I asked Tille to help me with the baby. She said we should just send Noak for her when the time came. I don't think that is necessary. I'm in no pain now. How will I know when I'm in labor?"

"You're probably right, but I do think the baby has dropped. You'll know when labor starts in earnest." Kjerstin chuckled.

"How?" Annika asked, feeling ignorant. Knowing was better than not knowing. She had to know what to expect.

Kjerstin looked about as if searching for an answer. Finally, she drew a deep breath, sat on the bed, and aimlessly patted Annika's hand.

"I asked a question," Annika said, impatiently prompting Kjerstin.

Kjerstin tittered nervously. "It's nothing to worry about. I've had children, of course, and I've been present at birthings. I've never brought a baby into the world on my own, but I could if the need arose. Just remember, each mother and child finds the way as nature intended."

"I'm so ignorant." Annika clutched Kjerstin's hand. "Thank you for being here."

"You can do this. You're young, strong, and healthy. That's what counts. When Noak comes in, I'll send him for Tille." Kjerstin stood. "I'm going to fetch water."

Annika's muscle tension eased, but the swollen discomfort remained. The more she relaxed, the groggier she felt. Hours later, she awoke, pulled on her coat, and slipped outside to visit the privy. When she returned, she was startled to discover Tille

145

already nestled in the rocking chair. Annika had passed her by without even noticing.

"So you're getting close?" Tille asked.

"Must have been a mistake," Annika said.

"We'll see," Kjerstin said. She and Tille exchanged knowing looks.

Despite Kjerstin's objections, Annika helped ready the table for the evening meal. Freshly baked bread had awakened her appetite. She escorted Tille to the table and slipped into her own seat as the family gathered.

They discussed harvest production and threats of a bad winter, but Annika's attention drifted, and fears whirled. Her appetite failed her, and she had difficulty eating. She hated not knowing what to expect. *If having a baby is a natural thing, exactly what does that mean?* Did it mean she didn't have to do anything? If she was supposed to do something, what was she supposed to do? Why was she unwilling to ask? *Why do so many die? It has to be horrible. What went wrong for Oscar's wife and child?* Her chest was tight. She had to start getting answers. A long drink quenched her dry throat and washed down her last bite as Kjerstin's voice drew her attention.

"Children, I want you to gather up whatever you need for tonight and for school tomorrow," Kjerstin said.

"We're going to camp out tonight at Oscar's cabin," Noak said. "I need to do some work over there tomorrow."

Tyko gave his father a knowing glance but said nothing.

"I love a campout," Kia said.

"Makes no sense to me," Annika said as she maneuvered from her seat. "I slept all afternoon, and I'm still tired." She gathered up leftover rolls and stored them in the cupboard. However, she was unable to retrieve the dishpan before a cramp pierced her like a knife and left her feeling weak. She grasped the back of Noak's chair and struggled to manage the pain without frightening the children.

Kjerstin sprang to her side and guided her to bed, where Tille fussed with pillows.

"I'll clear the table," Noak said. Directing his attention to Tyko and Kia, he said, "Go collect your things like Mor told you."

Annika knew hasty preparations were being made, but she was preoccupied. She clamped her jaw against the groan that rose to her throat.

"I must get food together for Noak," Kjerstin said. "When I get back, we'll get Annika ready for bed."

Tille nodded in agreement. She perched on the edge of the bed and unlaced and removed Annika's shoes. *What a relief*, Annika thought.

"Tyko!" Annika called out as he passed by on his way outside to help Noak. "Please move the rocking chair closer so Tille can have a proper place to sit."

Tyko did as she asked.

"Thank you!" Annika called after his departing figure.

"Are you sick?" Kia asked in a half-whispered voice as she peered into Annika's face. Her timid hand welcomed Annika's grasp.

"I'm not sick." When Kia's concern failed to fade, Annika explained, "I'll feel fine after the baby gets here."

"Ooh." Kia's eyes widened with wonder.

"Don't worry, because your mor and I are counting on you to help your far." She squeezed Kia's hand and sent her on her way. The last things Annika heard before she drifted into a fitful sleep were the back door closing and the team and wagon pulling away.

A gentle nudge at her shoulder prompted Annika to open her eyes. Kjerstin and Tille stared down at her.

"We're trying to decide if it is too soon to get you ready for what lies ahead," Tille said.

"I don't know about that, but I need to go to the privy," Annika said. She pushed herself into a sitting position.

"I brought in the commode." Kjerstin steered Annika to the seat tucked into the far corner of the room. "No need to be out in the night air."

Annika stepped lively to her destination. She readied herself for the task and sat down. Fluid gushed into the pail below. Frightened and confused, she stood when it was safe.

"Did your water break?" Kjerstin asked.

"I don't know. I thought I had to pee. I don't think I did. The pressure is gone. Is there any way to know?" Annika had many questions and no answers.

"Most likely," Tille said. "We'd better get you undressed."

"Undressed?"

The women directed Annika to bed and helped her disrobe.

"Can I put my nightgown on?" Annika asked.

"This will be more comfortable," Kjerstin said, producing a waist-length, sleeveless top that buttoned down the front.

The attire annoyed Annika, but she complied.

"We'll keep you covered," Kjerstin said. "There won't be much room for modesty in getting this job done. When that baby's in your arms, pain and embarrassment will be forgotten."

"I must lie down." Annika promptly covered herself. *No wonder they sent the family away.* She closed her eyes and pretended to rest. She wanted to be left alone. But concern about what else they might conjure kept her alert.

"I'll lay another fire. If the temperature drops, it will be too cold for a baby," Kjerstin said, and Annika heard her open the firebox door and add wood to the fire in the kitchen before she began work at the fireplace. "I'll light this later," Kjerstin told Tille. She ladled warm water from the reservoir into the wash pan to clean her hands and arms. "Do you want me to fix a basin for you?" she asked Tille.

When Tille finished washing, Kjerstin put the empty basin on the small table near the bed and fetched clean towels and washcloths.

Annika drifted into a troubled sleep only to be nagged

by her thoughts. Even in sleep, she couldn't escape. Her half-awake state dragged her back to New York City and that vile, despicable man. His disgusting laugh and leering eyes haunted her. Hateful words echoed. Confusion and distrust in Mrs. Brown's eyes made Annika's heart weep. Fleeting glimpses of Addie's compassion were the only comfort. Nothing wiped away his hateful actions. Never again would she allow it.

"No. No! I hate you. Get out!" she screamed. She awoke wide-eyed in a sea of fear and confusion. Her drenched shirt clung to her clammy body. Her throat felt raw.

Concern filled Kjerstin's and Tille's faces as their hands comforted her. Kjerstin wiped Annika's face with a warm, moist cloth and smoothed her hair from her face. Tille offered a drink. No one spoke. Cool, refreshing water steadied Annika's nerves, and she attempted to collect her wits.

"I ache," Annika said, "like an old fat toad waiting to pop."

"That sounds about right." Tille's raspy chuckle lightened the mood. "Having a baby is no easy business."

Tille inched the rocking chair closer, and Kjerstin fetched a chair for herself. The three women passed the time by speaking of family, friends, church, and handiwork. Annika felt safe. She trusted these women.

Her back and legs ached, but that was nothing compared to the intense spasm that gripped her body as if it had a life of its own. There was no enduring the pain; ending it was the only thing that mattered. She couldn't speak. Never had she expected this.

"That was a contraction," Tille said. The women washed again and sprang to action.

"Don't be frightened by the pain. All women have such pain. It will come and go and finally end." Kjerstin reassured Annika. "I can't tell you when. Each woman has her pace, and the baby sets the time."

"I need to know the baby's position," Tille said as she stepped closer to Annika.

"How can you?" Annika asked when pain permitted.

"I need to feel your belly. There is no certainty, but time and experience are good teachers." Tille warmed her hands and gently probed Annika's belly. "The baby is starting to turn." She laid a hand on the lower right side of Annika's belly. "The head is here." She placed Annika's hand over the baby's head so she could feel. "Next time, I'll look below. When I do, plant your feet flat on the bed, and bend your knees with legs apart." Tille's keen focus and concern reassured Annika. "Please do your best to follow my instructions; pain makes that difficult."

"I'll try," Annika promised.

"You're doing fine." The older woman patted Annika's hand.

Over and over, the women tended to increasingly harder rhythmic spasms that inched the baby to birth. The need for relief consumed Annika.

"Is this baby ever going to come?" she asked. Then, gaining confidence, she told herself, "I can do this."

Kjerstin mopped Annika's brow and urged her to persevere. The wee hours of the morning brought the final bout of contractions.

"Push. Push hard. He's doing his best to come—help him," Tille, who had long since stationed herself near Annika's feet, said.

"I am pushing as hard as I can. I can do no more."

"You must push harder," Tille said. "Kjerstin, scoot in behind her so she can push back against you. She needs more leverage."

Kjerstin did as Tille instructed.

"Keep pushing, Annika," Tille said.

"We're close. You can do this. Give it all you've got. Push," Kjerstin whispered in Annika's ear.

Annika pushed with all her might as if her life depended upon it, fearing that it did.

"I see the head. He's coming facedown. That's good. Lord willing, the baby will spill into life."

Annika was exhausted, but she would not let her baby down. She pushed as if her life and the baby's life depended upon it. Mamma had done it for her, and she would do it for her child.

"We're blessed. The head is clear. Now one shoulder. Now the other. It's done."

Annika fell back against the pillows, limp with fatigue, and welcomed the shrill wail that ended the monotonous struggle.

"Kjerstin, I need you," Tille said.

Annika watched Tille place the tiny newborn on the flannel blanket Kjerstin held. She tucked the blanket around the infant and laid him into his mother's arms. Annika gazed into the damp, wrinkled red face. Her breath caught in her throat. She lifted her eyes to Kjerstin with an unspoken question.

"He's all boy," Kjerstin said.

Annika slipped the blanket away and counted ten beautiful fingers and toes. Awe and gratitude engulfed her.

"You rest, and I'll bathe him," Kjerstin said as she tucked the baby back into warmth.

Annika's eyes followed her son until Tille called her back to completing the task at hand.

After freshening herself and donning her nightgown, Annika sat in the cushioned rocker and held Tomas. Entirely engrossed in her son, Annika barely noticed the older women cleaning her bed so mother and son could lie down.

A whimper and persistent nudge roused Annika. It took a moment before she realized Tomas was hungry. She pushed herself up into a sitting position in bed and unbuttoned her top. She maneuvered the baby's head into a comfortable position just below her breast. She whispered a prayer and coaxed the infant to respond. The older women discreetly watched from the table where they sat drinking coffee. Annika expected the task to be difficult, but she proceeded as if she knew exactly what she was doing. The first attempt failed. The second resulted in the baby latching on to her finger. When she pulled her finger away, his whimper grew to a cry. She tried again. This time, a droplet of milk oozed to the surface, and the baby hungrily latched on. She smiled. Only then did she notice Kjerstin and Tille beaming approval.

"How long should I let him feed?" Annika asked.

"The first few feedings will be short. Trust him to know when he's done," Kjerstin said, turning her attention to the opening door.

"Is it safe?" Noak asked with a teasing tone as he peeked around the door.

"Yes, yes. We have a new addition," Kjerstin said as Annika covered herself with the blanket.

"Did she have trouble?" Noak asked.

"Only normal trouble," Tille said.

While Noak chatted with Annika, Kjerstin poured him a cup of coffee. "How are you doing?" he asked.

"Scared, but better than I expected. I'll feel better in a day or two. Now I know why everybody left."

"And now we can relax. I'm pleased you are feeling well. I wanted to check on you and get a cup of coffee before I went to work." He turned to leave, and Annika shifted the baby into a sleeping position next to her.

"Better try to burp him first," Tille said.

"I forgot." Annika moved the baby to her shoulder and patted his back. She then nestled him back into bed, and they dozed.

Annika awoke to a muffled rattle from the kitchen. She checked the baby, propped herself up on pillows, and watched Kia help her mother with the evening meal. Annika wanted to help, but she doubted she had the strength. She was hungry and wanted to sit at the table. She sat up on the edge of the bed and cradled the baby in her arms. That was the invitation Kia needed. She made a beeline to Annika.

"Can I see?" she asked. "Can I hold him?"

Annika caught the hasty shake of Kjerstin's head. "Maybe when he's a little older. Right now, everything is new, and he wants to stay with Mamma." She brought the baby's hand out, and he clasped Kia's finger. She giggled with pleasure.

"Are you all better now?" Kia asked.

"Yes, I'm better," Annika said with a reassuring smile.

Kjerstin had already prepared the baby's bed, so Annika laid him down in the borrowed cradle and nudged it to rock slightly. She turned her attention to Kia. "Let's see if we can help your mor."

"No, you sit down right there." Kjerstin pointed to Annika's place at the table, next to where Tille was seated. "You'll pay a high price if you get too feisty too soon."

Annika lowered herself gently onto the hard bench, not knowing how long she could endure it.

The men washed up after chores, and Tyko marched to the cradle and took a long look at the baby before he came to the table. He smiled affectionately and asked, "How come he is so scrawny?" with a devilish twinkle in his eye.

"Well, aren't you a chip off the old block?" Annika said.

A shrill whimper called her. She scooped the child into her arms and cooed softly. She held him with one arm and turned the rocker away from the family, who were eating. She sat down and nursed the infant. When he slept, she returned him to the cradle and rejoined the family.

Before turning in for the evening, Annika opened Mamma's Bible to the family record pages. She carefully inked in *Tomas Isak Svensson* and *November 23, 1866*. In brackets, she added *Friday*. She stirred the air with her hand, and when she was sure the ink was dry, she laid the Bible aside and crept into the bed with Tomas. That night, Kia shared the big bed with Annika because Tille was staying for a few days to ensure that everything was off to a proper start.

## CHAPTER 14

# JUL

November faded into December as Annika was consumed with meeting Tomas's constant needs. Feedings, diapers, and interrupted sleep ruled her life. Despite her low energy level, she struggled to assist Kjerstin with the daily work routine.

> Marine Settlement
> December 1866
>
> Tomas is my world. But already I'm weary of feedings and diaper changings. Diapers hang everywhere. We rarely have company since Oscar left for the pineries. I miss him. Christmas is almost here—Tomas's first Christmas. Yesterday we decorated with pine boughs and evergreen. The aroma fills the cabin. Today Noak and the children went after branches of holly berries while Kjerstin and I cook. Family is good.

Annika returned the journal to its place on the trunk and checked on Tomas, who slept in his cradle. She hoped he would nap long enough for her to help with Christmas preparations.

The scent of evergreen mingled with the aroma of molasses boiling in a thick pan on the stove tickled her nose. She sat at one end of the table, behind a smooth, flat stone and a pile of walnuts. She held each walnut between her thumb and finger and gave it a sharp, quick rap with a hammer until she accumulated a small pile. She pulled the bits of shell away, removed the meats, and dropped them into the cup Kjerstin had provided. The work awoke bittersweet memories of Christmases past.

"How many will you need?" she asked Kjerstin, who worked with a large lump of dough at the opposite end of the table.

"A cupful at least. More is better." Kjerstin giggled as she put the dough aside. She was making cinnamon rolls, and hers were reputed to be the best in the territory. Kjerstin stepped to the stove to check the molasses. "I think this has boiled down enough. Butter that plate really good, and I'll pour it in. Maybe we'll get finished before they get back."

Kjerstin poured the gooey mixture onto the plate. Annika pulled on her coat and took the plate outside so the candy could cool. She deposited it onto a flat, crusty portion of snow drifted against the porch.

The crusted snow glistened as if God had scattered glittering jewels everywhere. The trees hung full with new-fallen snow. Had it not been so nippy, Annika would have lost herself in the beauty. Instead, she shivered and dashed inside. She smiled to herself as she thought about the children's reactions to the taffy surprise. Inside, she warmed herself at the fireplace and checked on Tomas before she returned to her task. Annika absentmindedly shelled nuts while she gave Kjerstin's baking keen attention.

Kjerstin's deft use of the rolling pin spread the dough to the thickness of a small twig. Then she liberally slathered freshly churned butter over the dough. She took the bag of brown sugar she had been saving since Noak's last trip to Stillwater and crumbled it generously over the dough. She searched the cupboard until she retrieved a tin container of spice. She freely sprinkled cinnamon across the entire surface of the dough. The aromas of butter, brown sugar, cinnamon, and molasses mingled with the scents of pine and evergreen. Annika's mouth watered as she watched Kjerstin coax the edge of the dough up, rolling it onto the remaining dough to form a long, thick roll. Kjerstin liberally buttered the sides and bottom of the bread pan and sprinkled walnut meats and the remainder of the brown sugar across the bottom. She cut the dough into one-and-a-half-inch slices and nestled each circle onto the bed of butter, sugar, and nuts. When the pan was filled, she covered it with a cloth and set it aside.

"When they are raised to twice that size, they'll be ready for the oven," Kjerstin said.

Tomas's whimper told Annika it was time for a diaper change and a feeding. She settled herself in the rocker. She loved the sense of purpose motherhood provided. She wanted Tomas to have the same sense of security she saw in Tyko and Kia. She knew her own sense of well-being had increased since she arrived in Minnesota—at least while she remained on the Andersen homestead. Without family, she had felt lost. Annika shook her head and refused to let her thoughts go there. She and Tomas would carry on the Svensson name in North America, as her parents had dreamed.

A rattle on the door latch rocked Annika from her daydream. She gathered the quilt tightly around Tomas, rose from the rocker, and strolled to the frosty window. The overcast sky made Annika wonder if it would snow. Kjerstin, bundled against the cold, retrieved the taffy perched in the snow. Kjerstin gave a wistful look to the east, and a smile brightened her face. Annika wiped frost from the window and squinted through the cleared glass. Her eyes darted to where Kjerstin directed her attention: distant figures trudged through the snow. Annika smiled and rushed to diaper Tomas so she could lay him in the cradle. She placed two more logs in the fireplace flames and lifted the trunk lid.

Annika knew the situation called for a warm fire, piping hot chocolate, and lots of bread and butter to accompany the stew. She rummaged among her possessions until she located the packet of cocoa she had brought with her from New York.

She and Mor used to share hot chocolate in their room on cold winter nights. She hadn't drunk cocoa since her mother's death. She heard Kjerstin stomp her feet outside the door before reentering. Kjerstin stepped onto the rag rug and wiped the remaining snow from her feet. Annika headed to the stove.

"I saw them. They'll be here shortly," Kjerstin said as she set the plate of taffy on the table and brushed the flecks of snow from the surface with a towel. "This set up good." She turned toward Annika. "What do you have there?"

"A Christmas surprise," Annika answered as she set a pan filled with milk on the stove to warm. She dumped a small mound of cocoa into a cup and began adding sugar. When she had the proper balance of sugar and cocoa, she set the cup aside. She set the butter bowl, a knife, and the bread board on the table and sliced bread. She then poured a small amount of warm water into the cocoa-and-sugar mixture, stirred until it was smooth, went to the stove, and gradually added the cocoa mixture to the warm milk, stirring all the while.

"That will warm them. It feels like the temperature has dropped. I hope it doesn't storm tonight. I want to attend church," Kjerstin said as she lifted the lid on the kettle and stirred the stew. During winter months, hot stew was always available for anyone toiling or traveling in the cold. Kjerstin removed the cloth from the cinnamon rolls and slipped them into the hot oven.

The aroma of baking cinnamon rolls greeted Noak and the children when they returned rosy-cheeked. Kjerstin quickly hushed the children so they didn't awaken the baby. Annika finished setting the table and helped Kia out of her damp clothing. She spread Kia's coat, shoes, and mittens on the hearth to dry in front of the fire. She offered to take Tyko's wet things as well, but he preferred to tend to his own things, as Noak did. When everyone was warmed through, they gathered at the table.

"Do you think the weather will hold so we can go to church?" Kjerstin asked Noak as she set bowls of stew on the table. "Annika is planning to take the baby for the first time. I hope it won't be too cold for him to go out."

"I'm thinking it is trying to clear off. We'll just have to see what tomorrow brings," Noak said as he signaled Tyko to return thanks. He then reached for a slice of bread and buttered it. "Do I smell chocolate?"

"That's Annika's Christmas surprise. I think she is saving it to go with our cinnamon rolls when they are baked," Kjerstin said.

"Mor and I sometimes shared cocoa in our room on cold winter nights. I want to share that with my new family. I hope I've prepared enough for now and later," Annika said as she poured hot chocolate. The family ate with hearty appetites.

"After supper, can we put out treats for the birds and squirrels?" Kia asked her mother.

"I'll help Kia with that," Noak told Kjerstin. "I have work to see to in the shop."

"Do you need help?" Tyko asked.

"Yes, I could use some," Noak said.

Annika brushed the bread crumbs from the cutting board into a small jar and crumbled uneaten morsels of bread on top of the scraps they had been saving all week. Then she gathered empty bowls and spoons and prepared the dishwater. If she was fortunate, she would get the dishes done before Tomas awoke.

Kjerstin opened the oven door a crack and peeked at her rolls. "They are almost done," she said as she stepped to the storage room and retrieved an ear of corn and a chunk of suet she had saved for Kia to hang for the birds.

While Annika washed dishes, she watched Kjerstin and Kia secure a long strip of rag to the corn cob so it could be suspended from a tree branch. Kia held her finger in place while Kjerstin tied the final knot.

"All God's creatures need to be remembered on this special night," Kia told Annika.

"That's right," Annika said as she handed Kia the bread crumbs.

"I'll empty the dishwater for you," Tyko said as he finished buttoning his coat to follow Noak outside.

"Wait for me!" Kia said as she struggled into her shoes and coat.

Within moments, Kjerstin and Annika were alone. Kjerstin stepped to the oven, removed the rolls, and turned them upside down on a clean cloth she had placed on the table. She waited awhile and then lifted the cooling pan from the hot rolls, revealing tasty, sugary, nutty rolls. Annika's mouth watered, and Kjerstin beamed.

Annika wanted to watch Kia, but Tomas's wail called. While she fed the baby, her eyes followed Kjerstin around the cabin as she distributed pointy-leafed holly branches bright with red berries among the pine and evergreen boughs. Then she placed several nearly used candles about the cabin—near but not among the boughs. Finally, she brought packages from her bedroom and placed them on the table.

Annika wished Tomas would finish nursing so she could collect her tokens.

"If he's finished, I'll change him if you need time before everyone comes back." Kjerstin held out her arms to receive the baby. "Would you please light the candles when you finish your chores?"

"Thank you." Annika transferred the baby and then knelt down beside her bed and pulled out a stash of all but one package. She added them to Kjerstin's collection. Annika pulled a small twig from the kindling pile and stuck it into the open flame until it began to burn. She used it to light candles. She had just extinguished the flame, when Kia bounded inside and stood in front of the closed door.

"Nobody can go outside. Far said so," Kia announced.

Kjerstin and Annika exchanged questioning looks as Kjerstin returned Tomas to Annika. Kia stood her ground but fastened her eyes on the small pile of gifts on the table. Kjerstin and Annika exchanged smiles. A sharp rap on the door drew Kia back to her mission. She snapped to attention and flung the door open.

Noak and Tyko inched through the open door, carrying a large object covered by a horse blanket. They set it down in the middle of the room and went back outside only to return with a smaller object covered by a horse blanket. Before Kia could close the door, Noak leaned outside, reached to the side of the door, and hauled in a broom. He nodded to Kia to close the door. Annika claimed the broom.

"Merry Christmas, Kjerstin," Annika said as she handed the store-bought broom to her.

"How? What?" Kjerstin was speechless. Everyone else smiled and enjoyed her surprise. "What a wonderful gift!" she exclaimed.

"I asked Oscar to pick it up for me." Annika answered Kjerstin's half-spoken question while Kjerstin gave the floor a few practice swipes with the broom.

"This will make sweeping a pleasure. Thank you, Annika."

"I can't top that," Noak said, "but I have finished our family's clothing chest." He pulled the blanket off the larger object and revealed a large two-door oak cabinet with two stacked drawers across the bottom.

Kjerstin opened the doors and revealed three deep shelves.

"I thought the children could each have a drawer for their clothing, and we can use the shelving in whatever way we think best," Noak said.

"It's beautiful and fine workmanship. This is wonderful," Kjerstin said before hugging Noak.

"He made this for you and Tomas," Tyko told Annika as he pulled the other blanket from the smaller object.

Now Annika was speechless as she held Tomas and caressed the smooth surface with her hand. This double-door cabinet was smaller, with side-by-side drawers on the bottom. Annika didn't know what kind of wood it was made of, but it matched her parents' trunk.

"You've done so much for me already." Annika felt the familiar lump rise in her throat. "I've never had my own piece of furniture. Thank you all." She moved her hand across the smooth wood grain and reveled in her good fortune.

"I think we'd better see to these young ones," Noak said, tousling Tyko's hair. He suggested everyone gather at the table.

Annika laid a drowsy Tomas in his cradle. "Of course we should," she said. "May I hand out my gifts?" She gave Kjerstin a tiny, thin packet. She handed Noak a bulky, lightweight bundle. She gave Tyko and Kia each two packages.

Kia tore a package open and discovered a tightly knit bright blue double-layer scarf and matching mittens. She squealed in delight. She ripped into the smaller package and found a tiny green flannel nightgown and a blanket for her baby doll. Kia bounded from her seat and fetched her doll from her bed. She watched the others as she dressed her baby.

Kjerstin turned her eyes to Tyko. "I'll go last since I have already received gifts. Open yours."

Tyko chose the large, flat package first. He uncovered a tablet without lines.

"Now you can collect your drawings and doodling all in one place," Annika said.

"A whole tablet for nothing but pictures?" he said. "This will keep me busy." He laid it aside and opened the second package, which held dark gray double-layer knit mittens and a matching hat. He modeled the perfectly fitting hat, wearing a silly smile. "Thank you," he said.

"I guess it's my turn," Noak said as he uncovered two pairs of knit socks and a muffler long enough to wrap around his neck twice. Annika had brought the yarn, which her mother had accumulated for a shawl she never made, from New York. "Thank you. These will warm me during Minnesota winters."

Kjerstin tugged at the paper that wrapped her second gift.

She found two freshly ironed white handkerchiefs with delicate white tatting around the edges. "These are beautiful. Did you make them?" she asked.

"Yes," Annika said, trying not to appear prideful. "Addie and Mrs. Brown taught me how to tat in the first weeks after Mamma's death. I made that top one when I was still in New York."

"I'll feel like a fine English lady when I carry these," Kjerstin said.

"Tyko and Kia, if you open those drawers in our cabinet, you might find something else." Noak's eyes twinkled, and his mouth twitched away a smile. "Tyko, yours is the top drawer."

Tyko stepped back as he watched Kia slide her drawer open. She reached in to pull something out, but it wouldn't come until Tyko gave the drawer another tug to open it wider.

"It's a cradle for my baby. Just like Tomas has." Kia set the cradle on the floor, ran to Noak, and showered him with kisses and hugs. "Thank you, Pappa." Then she was back kneeling beside the cradle and situating her baby in bed.

Tyko opened his drawer and found a slingshot and a bag of smooth stones for ammunition.

"I thought you would enjoy using that to practice aiming and training your eye for hunting. Your mor and I have decided you are old enough to accompany me on hunting trips," Noak said.

"Thanks, Pappa." Tyko centered a stone in the leather pouch of the sling and pulled back, testing the stretch in the strap. "Maybe I can give it a try tomorrow. It's too dark now." He was interrupted by Kjerstin clearing her throat.

"If we are ever going to get to my cinnamon rolls and Annika's cocoa, we're going to have to get this gift giving finished." She handed out her packages.

Kia tore the paper away to reveal a new dress with its own apron, and Tyko and Noak received matching flannel shirts. Then Kjerstin handed Annika a large bundle tied with a braided strand of yarn. Annika untied the bow and unfolded the bundle to discover a flannel-lined baby quilt with Tomas's name and birth date embroidered in the upper left corner.

"Now it's my turn to stammer," Annika said as she looked to Kjerstin in appreciation. "This is beautiful. How did you find the time to work on this without me knowing?"

"Tille and I worked on this to pass the time while you were trying to birth the baby. After that, we worked on it every time you took a nap. Then Tille took it home and finished it and brought it to me at church."

"Thank you," Annika said, feeling her eyes moisten.

"If you ladies will tell us where you want these cabinets, Tyko and I will set them in place while you see to the food," Noak said. As he spoke, he picked up one of the blankets and folded it. Tyko did the same with the other one.

"Put ours over there against the wall between the fireplace and Kia's bed. Both the children can get to it easily there," Kjerstin said. She turned to Annika and asked, "Where do you want yours?"

"Over against the inside wall by Tomas's cradle," Annika said, unsure of her decision.

By the time the furniture was in place, the cinnamon rolls and hot cocoa were waiting on the table. Everyone gathered around the table and enjoyed the Christmas treat.

"We can let these dishes wait until tomorrow," Kjerstin said as she gathered them and set them aside. "You children had better turn in. We'll be getting up early in the morning. Annika, will you help me prepare the Christmas goodies for Tille and the pastor before we turn in?"

Noak snuffed out the flame of each candle before he retired for the night.

◆

Annika slipped quickly from bed, lifted Tomas from his cradle, and nestled them back into bed. It was almost time for his early-morning feeding, and there was no need to awaken the entire household. He opened his eyes and smiled. She eased him against her breast, and he began to suckle. She lay half asleep, reliving their wonderful Christmas. That day, she would take Tomas to church for the first time. How would the other churchgoers treat her? She was anxious to get the trip done and behind her.

Kjerstin, whose shawl was tightly wrapped around her shoulders, interrupted Annika's woolgathering. She stooped and slipped large chunks of wood onto the fireplace coals and did the same to the cook stove. A few minutes later, she carried a long-handled brass bed warmer and an old empty cast-iron-covered kettle from the storeroom and placed them on the hearth near the fire. Soon everyone would awaken to warmth. Kjerstin filled the coffeepot with water and added coffee grounds. Annika rose from bed and snuggled Tomas back into his cradle. She went to the stove and began helping Kjerstin. Noak, fully dressed for work, gave Kjerstin a peck on the cheek and headed outside with milk bucket in hand.

"Do you think we could force the family to eat scrambled eggs and cinnamon rolls?" Kjerstin asked Annika with an impish grin.

"I could force myself," Annika answered.

"I'm going to hitch the team and get things ready," Noak said as he returned and set the milk bucket on the stool by the washstand.

While Kjerstin prepared the eggs, Annika filled the dishpan and washed last night's dishes. When breakfast was over, she would wash those dishes while Kjerstin got ready for church. Annika retrieved the bucket, and she and Kjerstin strained the milk. Annika poured two cups of warm milk. The remainder she poured into a crock, which she covered with a large plate and placed in the cupboard.

The aroma of coffee and eggs stirred the children from bed.

Tyko came down fully dressed for church. He wore his new shirt.

"Does the milking need done?" he asked through a sleepy yawn.

"No, but you could bring in a bit more wood so it will be waiting when we get back," Kjerstin said.

Tyko pulled on his coat and new hat and mittens and headed to the wood pile. There was already plenty of wood piled on the porch, but the family reserved that for use during blizzards, when visibility was limited and temperatures dropped. Annika helped Kia finish dressing and then slipped into her best dress. She tied a bib apron around her waist, returned to the kitchen, and poured coffee for the adults. When Tyko and Noak returned, the family gathered for a quick meal. Tyko offered prayer and mentioned their good fortune to have cinnamon rolls again.

"I'm ready, and I'll take care of the dishes," Annika told Kjerstin as she started gathering dishes. Annika had the dishes washed and dried in no time.

"Tyko," Noak called from his bedroom, "will you please pull the sleigh up to the porch? We'll be ready to leave shortly."

Tyko grinned because he loved adult responsibilities. He pulled on his outdoor attire and scurried out.

Annika hurried back to her area and readied Tomas for his first trip outside the cabin. She changed his diaper, checked to make sure his undershirt wasn't soiled, and pulled socks and booties onto his feet. Then she put two gowns on him. The first was a drawstring flannel gown she had made. The outer gown, a loaner from Tyko, was open at the bottom and trimmed with blue piping around the neck, wrists, and bottom.

"You are the most handsome baby in the world," Annika cooed to him as she fussed with his gown. The blue felt bonnet snugly fit Tomas, and Annika tied its ribbon beneath his chin. Tomas smiled and kicked his feet. "Does that little hat feel good over baby's ears?" Annika asked him. She picked him up and carried him about with her as she readied his blankets for his final bundling before they left. She lifted the trunk lid and slipped Tille's gift into her coat pocket. She heard the horses outside, laid Tomas in his cradle, and joined the family as they pulled on coats.

Tyko trudged inside with a couple of deer hides that had been sewn together. He dropped them in front of the fireplace and warmed himself. "Can I fill the warmers with coals?" he asked his mother.

"Yes, but be careful. Don't get burned," Kjerstin said as she turned her attention to collecting baskets for Tille and the pastor's family.

"Are we ready?" Noak asked. He turned to Annika and the baby. "You should come last. I'll come back to help you." With that, he stepped outside and began settling his family into the sleigh for the trip. Annika stepped to the window and watched.

First, Kjerstin went out with her goody parcels, and Noak settled her into a deep pile of hay. Next, he plopped Kia onto her mother's lap. He stepped back to the house, grabbed a blanket, and tucked it around Kjerstin and Kia.

Then he and Tyko began to talk. Annika couldn't hear them. Finally, Tyko climbed into the back of the wagon and sat down. Noak stepped inside and wrapped an old coat around the coal-filled bed warmer. He carried it outside, where he handed it to Tyko, who nestled it between himself and Kjerstin. Kjerstin flipped a portion of their blanket over the container. Noak returned inside and wrapped the coal-filled kettle in a piece of an old blanket. He set it on the opposite side of Tyko and then tossed his son the last blanket, and Tyko covered the container with part of it and nodded to Noak. Annika laid Tomas on the blankets she had prepared and individually wrapped each around him. Noak escorted them outside. Tyko spread the blanket across his legs and motioned to Annika to settle herself and the baby on the other side of the container. Tyko included Annika and Tomas under his blanket.

"We're set," Tyko said as he settled back against the side of the sleigh.

Noak retrieved the deer hides from the hearth and slipped his head through an upper opening between the two hides. Then he slipped his arms through the slits at the sides of the hides. He pulled the door securely shut, climbed into the seat, and signaled the team. With an easy jolt, the family were on their way.

Annika hoped the clear weather and the morning sun were good omens for Tomas's first day in church. The team kept a brisk pace, but the sleigh had high sides that served as effective windbreaks. Warmth emanated from the pot of hot coals.

"Is he warm enough?" Tyko asked.

Annika slipped her hand inside the blanket and confirmed Tomas was toasty warm before she responded. "He's doing fine."

The trip took less time than expected because the sleigh slid along easily on the packed snow. They stopped at Tille's house. Kjerstin handed Noak a goody basket to deliver. Tyko vacated his space so Tille would have something to lean against. He rewrapped their blanket so he could sit on the opposite side of Annika and Tomas.

"What a wonderful Lord's day we have," Tille said as Noak and Tyko helped her settle into her designated spot. Tyko tucked her blanket around her, and they were on their way.

"Thank you for the wonderful work you did on Tomas's blanket," Annika said as she leaned over and touched Tille's mitten-covered hand. Annika was relieved that Lota apparently had gone to her parents' church for Christmas services.

Several families had already gathered in the churchyard. Noak drew the horses to a spot near the door, and he and Tyko bounded to the ground. First, Noak lifted Tille to the ground and secured her blanket around her shoulders. Tyko helped Annika and the baby alight, and Noak helped Kjerstin and Kia. As the women made their way the short distance to the church,

Noak and Tyko fed the horses and spread blankets across the back of each animal.

Annika silently prayed for strength. She had been dreading this moment. But she had to keep a positive attitude. Maybe the goodness of the child and Jul season would soften hearts. Tille opened the door. When Annika stepped over the threshold, the chatter subsided. A dead hush fell over the women gathered in the front pews. Some of the men looked up to take note of the chill in the air before they resumed conversation. Annika stopped in her tracks, unable to move forward, until Kia's jostle from behind informed her that she was blocking the door. She forced herself to move. Tille stepped ahead of her.

"Isn't this your usual pew?" Tille asked as she settled herself next to Annika's usual seat and motioned for the young mother to join her.

Annika collapsed into the pew, and Kia and Kjerstin inched toward their usual seats.

"Folks who have known no heartache can forget their manners," Tille whispered. "Pay them no mind. Only the Lord can judge the heart."

What would she have done without Tille at her side? Annika made no effort to answer, because she was preoccupied with resisting the urge to flee. Would the pain of that horrible night ever end? Annika went through the motions of loosening Tomas's bonnet and blanket. She shut out the peering eyes.

"My, he has grown since I last saw him." Tille's reassuring whisper continued. "You have been doing well with him. He's pink and plump. He's a happy baby," she said as she caressed his cheek with a wrinkled finger.

Annika tried to smile. Then she remembered the tiny gift in her pocket. She pulled it out and presented it to Tille, who beamed. Tille unfolded the wrapping to uncover a freshly ironed lace-trimmed handkerchief.

"This is beautiful. Did you make it?"

"Yes, I made it for Mor's last Christmas. She put it away for a keepsake and never carried it. I want you to have it. You are a wonderful friend to me."

"Thank you," Tille said.

Annika heard a rustle of skirts and realized the women had turned to face the front. She heard a couple of older women greet Kjerstin. Noak and Tyko went to their usual seats. A low murmur returned to the front of the women's section. Annika failed to relax.

"The worst is over for now." Tille squeezed Annika's hand and turned her attention to the front.

Reverend Olander and his family arrived, and shortly, the song service began. Apparently frightened by the singing, Tomas wailed. Annika, humiliated again by the disruption, bundled Tomas and stepped outside with him. If it hadn't been so cold, she and the baby would have just waited in the sleigh, but she knew inside was the best place for Tomas. She could not avoid the situation forever. Misery engulfed her.

She didn't know the lone rider who dismounted, tied his horse's reins to the Andersen sleigh, and made his way to the door. When he addressed her, she jumped.

"Merry Christmas, Annika."

Her mouth was agape. "Oscar?" she asked. She barely recognized him with his long hair, full beard, and shaggy mustache.

"Hair provides warmth," Oscar said, enjoying her surprise. "I received word that Mother was ill, so I came down yesterday to check on my folks."

"Was it serious?" Annika asked. "Are your parents well?"

"Yes, she has a bad cold, but Dr. Randall is seeing to her. She gets to feeling blue this time of year. I think my visit cheered her. I'm headed back now. I stopped, hoping to see you." He reached into his pocket as Annika cuddled Tomas into her shoulder against the cold. "This is for you." He held in the palm of his hand a delicately carved heart. A narrow strip of tanned hide coiled around the trinket.

"It's beautiful. Did you make it? Oh, Oscar, seeing you is enough."

"I don't want you to forget me." Oscar slipped the necklace over her head.

"I wouldn't forget," Annika said. "I have a gift for you at home. I never expected to see you until spring."

"Some things just have to be done." Oscar pulled back the blanket and peeked into Tomas's face. "We'd better get inside. It's too cold out here for him."

He held the door, and Annika scurried inside and returned to her seat. Oscar stepped inside, and murmurs swept across the gathering. Annika, flush faced, stared straight ahead. Oscar paused and then stepped to the pew directly across from Annika and sat down. As a song was drawing to an end, Kjerstin, stern-faced, and Kia rose from their seats and joined Annika and Tille in the back. Reverend Olander delivered an uplifting Christmas message, and communion was observed.

After services, the congregation was slow to depart. Oscar rose to his feet and cleared his throat to gain everyone's attention. "I thought you might want a bit of news. Folks in Stillwater had a tragedy Christmas night. There was a fire in the center of town, on the block bounded by Myrtle, Chestnut, and Second streets and Union Place. The fire was confined to a one-block area, but a good section of it was leveled. There was considerable property damage, but as far as I know, no lives were lost."

While people gathered around Oscar and questioned him, Reverend Olander made his way to Annika and welcomed her and Tomas. Annika thanked him.

"I have a small token for your family," Kjerstin said, filling the silence. "I'll fetch it."

Annika followed Kjerstin outside. She climbed into the bed of the wagon and handed Kjerstin the last parcel of cinnamon rolls. She felt about in the hay only to discover the coal pot was cold. She snuggled Tomas against her and considered slipping him beneath her coat. By then, people were spilling from the church. Tyko made his way to the team, pulled a blanket from Blue, and wrapped it around Annika and the baby. The blanket was warm from the heat of the animal.

Annika smiled. "Thank you."

Tyko smiled and headed back toward his friends.

Annika fingered the wooden heart that dangled outside her coat.

Oscar climbed into the wagon and sat across from her. "It's wonderful to see you. The pineries have never been so lonely."

"I have missed you. Seeing you is such an encouragement." She glanced toward the church. "I believe it was colder in there than it is out here." She tried to joke, but her heart wasn't in it.

"They haven't been willing to get to know you. You'll win them over. If not, it's more about them than you," he said, and Annika tried to believe him. "I wanted to tell you Kjerstin invited me for dinner—I'd like nothing better. But I have to get back to camp before dark so I don't lose my way."

"Will you have time? What if it snows?" Annika felt apprehensive.

"I'll have plenty of time. If a blizzard blows in, I'll stay over in Taylors Falls until it's safe to travel." He leaned forward and whispered, "Consider yourself kissed until I find a more appropriate time and place." He squeezed her hand and took one last peek at Tomas.

He stood and steadied first Tille and then Kjerstin as Noak helped them into the sleigh. Then he received Kia and sat her next to her mother. He sprang to the ground, shook hands with Tyko and Noak, mounted his horse, and was gone.

Annika watched until he disappeared around the bend in the road. Tyko wrapped the second blanket around Kjerstin and Kia. He sat down beside Annika, who offered him a portion of her blanket, which he didn't refuse.

"Pay them no mind," Tille told Kjerstin. "Some folks' hearts are harder than others', but God's will is always done."

"You're right. My problem is keeping myself in check," Kjerstin said.

Annika wanted to join in, but she knew her words would be too harsh. Instead, she turned her thoughts to her good fortune to see Oscar. Maybe she could endure this terrible time. She knew her future there depended upon her strength.

Noak helped Tille from the sleigh and accompanied her to the door. Annika was puzzled when he followed her inside. Tyko leaned over and said, "He's making sure her fire is going good. It won't take long." He was right, and before long, the family were on their way again.

## CHAPTER 15

# THE LETTER

Annika listened as Noak read Miss Addie's letter to Kjerstin. The content of the letter had so stunned Annika that she wanted her cousins' reactions. Kjerstin frequently interrupted and questioned Noak in Swedish about the meaning of what he read. Annika tried to be patient.

New York City
January 1867

My dear Annika,
I hope this finds you and your family in good health. I hold you in my heart and think of you often.

I risk awaking painful wounds because I have important news: Walter Brown is dead.

A deputy sheriff came to the Browns' home at two in the morning to inform Ruth. She has made no comment to me about the incident. The *New York Times* printed an article that stated Brown was stabbed in the belly during a barroom brawl. No charges were filed because it was ruled self-defense. Folks say he was drunk and assailed someone's wife. Mrs. Brown deserved better. Her parents tried to tell her. Their son has taken over running the shipping company.

After private funeral services, Ruth and the attorney began settling Walter's affairs. She found proof of his disgusting behavior with you and previous employees. She came to me with questions, and I told her exactly what I knew.

Ruth isn't well. She is overcome with guilt and seldom goes out. I have heard her up pacing at night. She questions how she could have been so blind and stupid. She worries that you harbor hard feelings toward her. This is the second reason I write. She asked me to.

She wants to open her home to you and the child. She believes it's her responsibility to rectify the damage Walter inflicted. She wants to provide for the child's education. She also remembers your dream of having a seamstress business, which she believes would thrive here.

I have been unable to sway her from these ideas. I hope she will be more responsive to a letter from you. I agreed to write because I was convinced she would proceed on her own if I failed to intervene. I regret any despair this may cause.

With fond regards,
Addie

Annika had read and reread the letter since Reverend Olander delivered it at the request of the postmaster at Marine Settlement. The news was unsettling.

Again, Noak paused and spoke to Kjerstin in Swedish. Kjerstin's expression told Annika that she too was bewildered.

"This Addie—she is the woman who sat with me in the garden?" Noak asked.

"Yes. She worked for Mrs. Brown's parents and cared for

Mrs. Brown from infancy. When they passed, Addie came to cook for Mrs. Brown. Addie loves Mrs. Brown as if she were her own child. She must be very worried."

"Will you go to her?" Kjerstin asked. Her strained voice and drawn expression touched Annika. She knew Kjerstin wanted to say more.

"I don't know. I don't know what to think," Annika said as she rose to tend to Tomas. She first changed his diaper and then nursed him. Holding Tomas comforted her.

Noak and Kjerstin talked together about the letter until mother and son joined them. Kjerstin set a cup of coffee in front of Annika. They shared their coffee but not their thoughts.

"I need some fresh air," Annika said. "Would you please mind Tomas while I take a walk?"

"Of course," Kjerstin said, taking Tomas.

Annika set her cup in the empty dishpan as she passed. She pulled on her coat and knotted a woolen scarf beneath her chin. She pulled on mittens and stepped outside. The brisk February breeze nipped her face. Sunlight sparkled on the snow, but Annika, deep in thought, barely noticed.

Brown was dead—murdered in a barroom brawl. *Poor Mrs. Brown. How could he do that to her? How could he do it to me?* Hot anger rose and collided with the cold, severe wilderness. The wind whipped at the tears that spilled down her cheeks. She swiped her mittens across her face and picked up her pace. She didn't stop until she reached the bridge. Only then did she realize she was tired. She stared into the barren trees that lined the creek banks. The stark contrast of the dark trees against the bright white snow cleared her thoughts. Why couldn't life's choices be as clear? Everything she thought was a cloudy, dirty gray. Then her thoughts whispered, *Stop worrying about Brown. He's dead.* Annika wondered if her shudder was one of relief or fear. Now Brown's fate had fallen to the judgment of God.

She hadn't intended to walk so far. She trudged back up the

hill to respond to Addie's letter. What could she say or do to help a woman so many years her senior? Yet Miss Addie believed she could help. She also had to give Kjerstin an answer. Again, she was alone without an understanding of what to do. Could she decide? *If only Oscar were here.*

Annika kicked her feet against the step, and snow fell from her shoes. She climbed to the porch and stepped onto the rag rug just inside the door. She removed her shoes, put them on the hearth to dry, and pulled on another pair of socks. She peeked at Tomas, who slept with the peace of an infant. Annika envied him.

She sat down at the table with Noak and Kjerstin. "Tell me what you think," she said.

"It's a burden for one so young," Kjerstin said.

"There was urgency in your mother's letter when she wrote to us. Then Miss Addie spoke of her concern for your safety. I never considered anything like this." Noak raked his fingers through his thick blond hair and motioned to Kjerstin for more coffee.

"What do you think I should do?" Annika directly addressed Noak.

"You must decide," Noak answered. "We tried to guide you about marriage, but you resisted because it wasn't right for you. You are young, but you know your own mind." He paused and looked into Kjerstin's eyes as if seeking support, and she gave him a slight smile. He leaned back and watched her fill his cup and also fill cups for herself and Annika before she sat down. "You have shown yourself to be responsible, capable, and seldom rash or impulsive. We trust you to make the right decision for yourself and Tomas."

"We are family," Kjerstin said. "You are welcome here for as long as you choose to stay. We will remain family, whatever decision you make."

Her voice was calm and even, but Annika read the message in her eyes: *Don't go. Please don't go.*

Annika stirred sugar into her coffee. "The letter will be hard to write. Will you read it before I mail it?" she asked.

"If you wish," Noak said.

"It will require some long, hard thinking," Annika said as she slipped the folded letter into her apron pocket and rose for a late start on the afternoon chores. "The children will be home soon, and I've disrupted our entire day."

Annika looked forward to the hum in the cabin when the children returned from school. The sounds of family comforted her. Tyko had grown into a considerate young man. Kia was blossoming with newfound confidence as she mastered the alphabet and numbers. These people were her family. Annika knew she could never return to New York.

They shared a quiet supper. Then Kia sat at the table and completed her homework under Annika's watchful eye while the women washed dishes. Noak and Tyko carried in extra firewood to fill the wood box to overflowing.

◆

The day's news had taken a toll. Annika had looked forward to turning in early and getting a good night's rest, but sleep eluded her. She raised her head from the pillow and listened intently. Was that Tomas's whimper? She tossed and turned without finding rest. The letter tromped through her thoughts and challenged her to do battle. Finally, she surrendered.

She arose from bed, pulled on a heavy sweater, collected pencil and paper, lit the candle on the table, and sat down. A blank sheet of paper lay in front of her, and Addie's letter lay nearby. She set her jaw. She would not rush into filling the page. False starts wasted paper. She would be sure of each sentence before she began.

She wrote, "Marine Settlement, Minnesota, February 1867," at the top of the page. *Whom should I write to?* she wondered. Miss Addie had written, and it seemed fitting to write to her. Annika thought about how to word the letter. Each option was awkward and confusing, regardless of how she arranged the words. Annika snatched Addie's letter and read it for the hundredth time. That was when she realized Addie was asking her to write to Mrs. Brown. That made sense. Mrs. Brown was overwrought and needed help. Annika carefully wrote, "Dear Mrs. Brown." *Now what?*

She decided she must write from her heart and tell Mrs. Brown she was sorry for her loss. She would apologize for not telling the woman about her husband's betrayal. Annika worded four sentences that came from her heart. She read them once and then twice. She stretched and yawned. She was exhausted. She gathered her materials, blew out the candle flame, checked Tomas's blankets, and turned in for the second time.

The next morning, Annika reread the letter. For the next several evenings, after everyone was in bed, she struggled with proper wording for each sentence until the letter was finished. Each morning, she reread the letter with a critical eye. Writing in small pieces made thinking easier. It kept conflicting ideas and feelings from crushing down on her. Still, she wondered how her letter could help Mrs. Brown.

Annika sat on her bed and reread the entire letter for what she hoped would be the last time. When she finished, she knew she had written the only letter she could write. She hoped it was good enough to help her friends so far away. She laid the letter aside and rose to finish her chores.

"I've finished my letter," Annika told Noak and Kjerstin as they ate their noon meal. "I would like you to read it."

"Now is as good a time as any," Noak said. His eyes questioned her when she didn't promptly produce the letter.

Annika retrieved the letter from her trunk and handed it to them.

Marine Settlement, Minnesota
February 1867

Dear Mrs. Brown,
My thoughts are with you. I pray passing time
will lessen your pain. I know the confusion you
must feel. Betrayal shows no mercy. Forgive me
for not coming to you about your husband. I
wanted to spare you.

At one time, maybe he was worthy of your
love, but his actions reveal something else. I
harbor no ill will toward you. You have no part
in his guilt. He alone is responsible. You were
always fair and caring toward me and my mor.
I am grateful.

I have a new life here. Each day, I let go
of a bit of the pain that brought me here. The
past has schooled me with harsh lessons, but
now I look to the future. I implore you to let it
go—as difficult as it may be. Anger, sorrow, and
loss are heavy burdens, but there is strength in
hope. I had to speak of my heartache if I was
to live in truth and honesty. I urge you to talk
to those who love and care for you. They will
listen without scorn or judgment. Miss Addie
has known you all your life. Let her help.

I cannot return to New York. I wish to raise
my child in the Swedish traditions of my parents.
Here I have family to help me do that. Thank
you for your willingness to pay for the child's
education, but that isn't necessary. I demanded
Mr. Brown provide for the child's education and
for my travel expenses, and he did so. I hold to
my dream of opening a seamstress shop, but

it must wait. First, I must establish myself and provide for my child.

I am indebted to you for your help. I wish only the best for you. Please give my best wishes and warm regards to Miss Addie, and thank her for writing.

A friend always,
Annika

Annika held Tomas on her lap, using her finger to play peekaboo. She cooed to him and twirled her pointer finger in the air. When she had his attention, she quickly hid her finger from his view. He grasped it in his hand when it reappeared, and Annika repeated the cycle. Tomas's blue-eyed gaze fastened to her smiling face, and he giggled as he grasped her finger.

Noak read the letter aloud while they played. When he was finished, he laid the letter on the table. Kjerstin's face reflected her pleasure. Annika broke the silence when neither spoke.

"I tried to be kind. There were so many things I could have said. But no one can change what is past. Not even Mrs. Brown." Annika heard herself talking, but she really didn't know what to say. She wanted them to tell her she had written the right thing, but how were they to know? "Do you think it will help Mrs. Brown?"

"It helped me." Kjerstin spoke first. "I am happy you will stay. I was afraid you would go because folks are so cold to you."

"That will follow me wherever I go," Annika said, hearing the anger she tried to conceal. She turned to Noak, waited, and then prodded. "Please tell me your view. Is this all right?"

"I see no wrong in the letter, if that is what you mean," Noak said. "I don't know if there is any way to know what is right in this matter. Have you written the things you wanted her to know?"

"Yes. I care for Mrs. Brown. She knew nothing of his hateful actions. She could have changed nothing even if she had known. He was wrong. But I need to know if this is what needs to be written."

"I understand wanting to know that you are doing the right thing," Noak said. "It reminds me of how I felt when Kjerstin and I decided to come to America. We considered it for a long time before we decided. Then we went to our parents to talk with them. I don't know about Kjerstin, but all I wanted to hear was that we were doing the right thing."

"Me also," Kjerstin said.

"Our parents couldn't tell us that. They wanted us to stay, but they understood the reasons why we had to go. There was no land for us. There were no jobs, and we had no way to support a family. They understood, but they were our parents, and they wanted us near." He reached for Kjerstin's hand. "It was hard for everyone. I took comfort in my far's words: 'It is your life, your decision, and I believe you will succeed.'" Noak ran his fingers through his hair. "This letter you have written is your decision. Is it something you can stand behind without regrets? If so, then you have done well. No one else can tell you if you have written the right or wrong thing. Only your own heart knows."

"That is frightening," Annika said. "Being a child is an easier life. But now I have a child of my own. I must change."

"Annika, may I ask why you have said so little about your life here and about Tomas?" Kjerstin asked.

"I wanted to write about my life as it was there. Brown destroyed her life and my life because he thought of no one but himself. I started feeling better only after I realized he was wrong and that only he was responsible. I think Mrs. Brown needs to understand that. I think telling her about my life here would distract her from her own life. I have cut my ties and made a new start. I think she needs to do the same. It isn't easy, and I sometimes wonder if it will ever end."

"I don't know about that," Noak said, "but I know you are

no longer the frightened young girl I brought home from New York."

"Will you post the letter for me?" Annika asked him.

"Yes," he answered, and they rose and returned to their work.

## CHAPTER 16

# REPENTANCE

Lota and Tille, who had ridden to church with the Andersen family, had been first ones out of the sleigh when they arrived. They were already inside, and Annika straggled along behind the Andersens. A hostile March gale ripped at Tomas's blanket. With her head down, Annika pushed toward the church building with Tomas's face nestled into the protection of her coat. Bright sunlight whispered the approach of spring, but the brisk wind warned, *Not yet.* Annika was anxious to get inside. The last thing Tomas needed was another earache. She stepped inside and sat in her customary seat, the last pew of the women's section, where Kjerstin and Kia waited. She removed her scarf and unbuttoned her coat, revealing the carved heart necklace she wore. Tomas played with it.

Annika's maternal smile faded when she saw Lota's scowl. She avoided eye contact, leaned toward Kjerstin, and whispered, "Have I done something wrong?"

"What?" Kjerstin asked.

"Never mind," Annika said, flipping the blanket around Tomas as she felt a draft from the open door that admitted latecomers. A tap on her shoulder and a stern whisper surprised her.

"I want to talk to you outside," Lota said.

Annika gave Tomas to Kjerstin, secured her scarf, and wrapped her coat closed. She followed Lota outside.

"Where did you get that necklace?"

"It was a gift," Annika answered.

"You know what I mean. Who gave it to you?"

"A friend."

"You don't have to act so smug, you little hussy. I know that necklace came from Oscar. Why can't you admit it?"

"Oscar gave me the necklace, and he is a friend," Annika said.

"You have such nerve to come worship with decent people. Don't you know you aren't welcome?" Lota said.

"Church is for sinners. I think I belong here," Annika said, wishing she would let herself slap the woman. She resented being spoken to in such a hateful tone.

"Just remember your place," Lota sputtered as she turned away and went back inside.

Annika knew Lota was jealous, but she couldn't understand why Lota was so hostile. Maybe she just needed someone to blame. Annika knew those feelings well. She couldn't change Lota, but she could try not to be mean-spirited. Besides, she didn't want the day to begin on a sour note.

Inside, Tomas leaned toward her and hugged her neck as she took him back and sat down. Annika's heart softened as she sang. Lota sat with her back ramrod stiff as she sang. Annika slipped the necklace underneath her dress—she saw no reason to antagonize.

Reverend Olander concluded his sermon by inviting anyone in the congregation who felt a need to walk closer to Jesus to come during the final hymn. Annika had listened attentively to the sermon, but she still wasn't prepared. Regardless of whether she was fully prepared or not, she would honor the commitment she had made. She lifted Tomas from her lap and gave him to Kjerstin, who looked to her questioningly. Annika stood and stepped into the center aisle before her nerve failed her. Did the singing congregants hesitate, or was it her imagination?

Reverend Olander stepped to the aisle and waited for her to join him. Her mouth was dry, and she silently pleaded for strength. His hand on her shoulder told Annika there was no turning back. She and Reverend Olander sat on the front pew and spoke in hushed tones. An occasional murmur from the congregation was the only other sound. Annika's trembling hands rested on her lap and clutched the handkerchief her mother had given her for her thirteenth birthday. Reverend Olander stood and faced the congregation.

"Annika has come today to seek God's providence in her life. She has been a believer since childhood but says she has not lived as Christ directed. She has asked to speak on her own behalf. Please listen with open hearts."

Annika somehow summoned the strength to stand and face the congregation. Reverend Olander took a seat nearby.

Annika searched for her voice. Fear thumped in her chest. Again, murmurs rippled across the group. She had to end the murmuring. She drew a jagged breath, but her voice failed. She swallowed and uttered her first raspy words.

"I've made mistakes. What I regret most is being dishonest with family and with you." Annika nervously shuffled her feet. "I'm thankful Noak and Kjerstin opened their home to me after Mamma died, though they knew nothing of my circumstances. I regret the pain I've brought to them." Her eyes found Tyko, and she remembered the anger she had seen in his eyes. "It was hard to talk about my past, so I didn't. My parents told me that truth may be hard to speak, but it is easier to carry than the burden of a lie. I found out what that meant when I decided to trust Noak and Kjerstin.

"I've lived here with secret sin and blamed you for not understanding. It was the best I could do at the time. Now I know I was wrong. I tried to trust people in New York, but it brought only pain. I was shunned and ridiculed. That is what I expected here. I was ashamed, so I hid at home. Noak and Kjerstin tried to help me, but I was stubborn. I judged you just as I believed you judged me." Her voice quavered, and she stopped. "I gave no explanation and blamed you for not caring."

Annika dabbed her eyes and blew her nose. "Not long

ago, I got a letter from New York." She paused to steady her nerves. She watched Noak rise, come forward, and sit beside Reverend Olander. Despite the sob-choked edge in her voice, she continued. "The letter contained news that my son's father had died." The quiet sanctuary grew still. "I will tell Tomas only that his father died.

"I want to make a new life here, but I can't do that under a cloud of suspicion. If I want your respect, I must earn it with honesty."

Nothing would change if she failed to finish. Annika had to make a stand for herself and for Tomas. He was an innocent child, and she couldn't allow him to be treated harshly because of her. She cleared her throat, forced herself to look across the congregation, and continued.

"The man who died was my employer. In New York City, there is little respect for immigrants. Maybe he thought he was entitled. I don't know." A long silence hung as she searched for words. "He took liberties I did not extend." She paused again. "Surely this is plainspoken enough for adults." Annika's voice broke. She examined the crevices in the plank floor beneath her feet.

She lifted her eyes and continued. "His own deplorable behavior led to his death. Now his actions are in God's hands, and I'm relieved to leave them there. Living with insult changes life in unbearable ways." Annika's eyes rested on Tomas, who sat quietly in Kjerstin's lap. She saw that Kjerstin wept, and moved by Kia's worried expression, she gave the child a reassuring nod. Annika's heart softened. "What nags me is that an innocent child may suffer for matters beyond his control. I implore you to accept Tomas without judgment. Please allow your children to play with him when the opportunity arises."

Annika heaved a heavy sigh. "I'm so tired. Guilt and shame are heavy burdens. I can't carry on alone. I need to let Jesus be a stronger presence in my life. I need the love and help of family and friends. Please help me find a better way." Tears streamed down Annika's cheeks. She sank onto the front pew, empty.

Noak hastened to her and rested his arm on the back of the pew. He leaned near and said, "Annika, I feel proud. Your strength and good sense are a powerful example of belief in God."

Annika quietly wept all the more.

"May I speak?" he asked her.

Annika nodded without looking up.

Noak stood and surveyed the gathering before he spoke. "I am encouraged by the decision Annika has made. Kjerstin and I have read the letter she received. She could have said more about this man, but she has shown the good grace to say less. As she said, these matters rest in God's hands. She wants to make a life for herself and her son. I hope you will extend her the privilege of a second chance." He put a hand out to her. "Annika, will you join me as we stand for a word of prayer from Reverend Olander?"

Annika drew comfort from the warmth and strength of his hand clasped around hers. Her once wobbly legs began to feel normal. Love and relief flooded her heart as she listened to the prayer offered on her behalf.

Noak affirmed Reverend Olander's amen, and the service concluded, but no one moved. Each person waited for the next one. Embarrassed and uncomfortable, Annika turned to Noak, who gave her shoulders a reassuring hug. She looked toward the pew where Lota sat stone-faced. Tille stood, squared her shoulders, and established eye contact with the women surrounding her. She excused herself and came toward the front. She grinned as she extended a warm hand of fellowship to Annika.

"That's how it's done, child. The hard times you have endured sadden my heart. The blessings of our Comforter go with you."

"You are a treasure." Annika welcomed the words of encouragement. People began to stir.

"I'm glad we're family," Tyko, who hovered close to Noak's side, said.

Annika noticed Ander Jansson approaching. He greeted Tyko.

"I'm sorry I said bad things about Annika, and I'm sorry I fought you," Ander said as he offered to shake Tyko's hand.

Annika beamed. Already, good had come from her decision.

Ander turned to Annika. "Tomas is a good baby, and I won't treat him mean."

Annika's eyes brimmed with tears. "Thank you," she said as she watched the boys head outside arm in arm. She was distracted by a thump and a hug.

"Please don't be sad." Kia's words were muffled by the gathers of Annika's skirt.

Annika knelt in front of Kia and grasped her shoulders. "These tears make me look sad, but they are happy tears because I asked God to help me make things better. That's a good thing."

"Are you sure?" Kia said.

"Yes. Please don't worry." Annika embraced the child, gave her a kiss, and stood.

Tille patted Kia's head. Tomas leaned to his mother, and Annika welcomed the reassurance of having him in her arms. Kjerstin hugged both Annika and Tomas.

"We will try to be better friends," Molly Jansson said as Annika's eyes met hers. Olle stood close by and shook hands with Noak as Molly continued. "We had no idea such terrible things could happen. I admire your courage."

Olle nodded in agreement. Annika noticed Lota and the majority of the congregation had left, and she realized there was still a long way to go.

"Thank you," Annika said in a timid voice.

"It's good of you to encourage Annika." Kjerstin interceded,

speaking to Molly. "I'm glad the boys have made peace."
Everyone smiled.

"We should go," Olle said. "We'll see you next week!" he
called back as they headed toward the door.

Reverend Olander and his wife came to Annika, and Mrs.
Olander wrapped her in a hug.

"Such unhappiness you have endured. I'm sure you have
done the best you could. I will offer more encouragement," Mrs.
Olander said.

"I've seldom seen that kind of fortitude from adults,"
Reverend Olander said as he shook her hand. "Your decision
made your parents proud. Please let me know if there is anything
we can do."

"I will," Annika said.

The church building was empty except for those gathered
with Annika. It was time to go home and see what tomorrow
would bring. Reverend and Mrs. Olander walked the short
distance to their home, and everyone else climbed into the
Andersens' sleigh, where Lota waited in the corner opposite
Annika.

## CHAPTER 17

# RENEWAL

Annika snuggled into the warmth of her comforter. Everyone else slept. A month had passed since they had attended church or gone anywhere. The promising sunshine of spring had long since faded into a nasty winter cold spell that had settled in the Hay Lake area. Two major snowstorms had dumped two feet of snow on the ground. Annika was thankful to be with the Andersen family, who knew how to survive severe weather.

When they'd returned from church that day, they had taken turns hauling wood first to the wood box in the kitchen and then to the pile alongside the fireplace hearth. Finally, they'd piled wood on the back porch, as high as Noak and Kjerstin could reach. Even so, Noak fretted about having enough wood to withstand below-zero temperatures.

Noak and Tyko had laden in supplies for the animals in the barn. They'd moved the chickens from the henhouse into the dugout lower level of the barn, where they would be better protected. Noak had cut a hole in the floor of the storage shed above the barn so he and Tyko could enter the lower level by ladder without having to wade downhill through snowdrifts.

In Marine Settlement, there were no snowplows or people to hire to scoop a path, as there had been in New York City. Noak had secured a rope from the cabin door to the west door of the storage shed, where a head-high windbreak kept snow from drifting to block the door. He also had secured a rope from the back door to the privy, but intense cold and deep snow had long since forced the family to rely on the commode tucked into the far corner of the cabin's storeroom.

Annika pushed herself up onto her elbow and looked through the heavily frost-coated windowpane near her bed and shuddered. Snow was falling for the fourth day straight. Wind howled around the corner of the cabin and ripped through the trees. Last week's ice storm had crashed tree limbs to the ground. She recalled how the noise had awakened Tomas and sounded as if the earth had split open.

Despite their being snowbound, the afterglow of her new beginning held. She slept well and no longer had to drag herself through the day. She popped up from bed, plucked Tomas from his cradle, and snuggled him into the warmth of her bed. Tomas awoke but drifted back to sleep while nursing. Annika loved the solitude of early morning. She dreamed of the future and hoped Oscar, so far away, was warm and safe. She wondered what spring would bring. Then her thoughts shifted to work. She was determined not to rely on the good graces of the Andersens indefinitely.

She wanted to stay in Marine Settlement, even if there were no wealthy families who needed a maid or seamstress. She groaned. How would she support herself in this frontier where perseverance and self-reliance were prized? If she wanted the respect of her neighbors, she had to earn it.

Sewing was her only talent. Kjerstin had been right when she said there was little call for a seamstress in those parts. Annika never doubted her decision to stay in Minnesota, but she had to find a way to stand on her own. She wasn't afraid of hard work. She had helped support her family since she was ten. She hated feeling dependent and indebted. She couldn't consent to marrying Oscar until she found a way to provide for herself.

She forced her thoughts back to the unanswerable question: *How can I begin a sewing business here?* There had to be a way. But what was it?

*Wait. Do I know there is no call for seamstress skills? No.*

*I have to try before I convince myself it cannot be done.* It was simple. Why had it taken her so long? Mrs. Brown had relied on Annika for darning and mending when she realized her stitching skill. What about men like Oscar, who had no one to tend to their mending and laundry, or older women like Tille, who were less able than they had once been? She would begin by offering laundry and mending services and work toward establishing a seamstress shop.

She'd use the winter shut-in time to sew items that demonstrated her skill. When spring arrived, she would attempt to place the items at the general stores in Marine Settlement, Taylors Falls, and Stillwater. Surely there were a few wealthy folks in the area. She'd begin with baby items. Even frugal, humble people were occasionally willing to purchase something special for a new addition. Annika's thoughts churned with ideas and items she could make from scraps she had accumulated. She could knit booties, mittens, and sweaters. She could tat trim around handkerchiefs for beautiful ladies. Lord willing, one day someone might ask her to sew a custom-made dress. Enough small steps would lead to her final goal, and her dream would be realized. The first step was to begin.

Annika eased herself from bed and tucked blankets securely around Tomas. She put pillows between him and the edge of the bed before she pulled on her dress and a heavy sweater. She added wood to the smoldering coals in the fireplace. When they began to burn, she moved to the cook stove, stoked the coals in the firebox, and waited for flames to lick the dry, hard wood. Soon the cabin was filled with warmth. She filled the coffeepot with water, added coffee, and set it on the stove to steep.

Annika was slicing the last of the pork belly, when Kjerstin, wrapped in a shawl, wandered in from the bedroom.

"Aren't you the early bird?" Kjerstin said.

Annika knew the continual confinement was wearing on Kjerstin's nerves. She placed a cup of hot coffee in front of her friend and gave her an encouraging smile. "I awoke feeling good," Annika said. "Are you sick?"

"Yes, sick of snow, ice, and gray days." Kjerstin sipped her coffee.

"Have you ever thought about trying to sell your cheese or your cinnamon rolls? Everyone in the territory talks about how good they are. I bet you could sell them for special occasions or even sell bread at the general store."

"I'd feel funny charging friends for things I have made."

"I don't see why. In New York, nearly every neighborhood had its own bakery. There are folks, like Tille and Oscar, who might prefer to purchase something rather than make it. No one could support themselves that way, but it would be additional income."

"I never thought of it like that."

"I'm going to use this time to sew babies' and children's clothes, and I'll try to sell them in the stores this spring. How can I know there is no call for seamstress work until I try?"

The side meat sizzled as Annika slipped it into the hot skillet. She opened the oven door and checked on the corn bread she was warming. When the meat was ready, she would use the drippings for a skillet of gravy. She couldn't allow Tyko and Noak to go out into the cold without a hot breakfast. Annika poured herself a cup of coffee and sat across from Kjerstin.

"I'm going to register Tomas's birth at the courthouse. He's an American citizen, and I want an official record. Then I'll make arrangements for my own citizenship. I've put the past behind me. It's time for a new start."

"I love having you here with us," Kjerstin said.

"I always want to be part of this family," Annika told Kjerstin impulsively, squeezing her hand.

The aroma of corn bread lured the family from sleep, and everyone, even Tomas, gathered for the morning meal. Noak, concerned about the restless animals and intense cold, refused Kia's plea to accompany the men to the barn.

"I could use help with Tomas this morning," Annika said, winking at Kjerstin, as she left the table to tend to the baby. Noak and Tyko readied themselves for the freezing weather and chores. Kjerstin stared into her coffee cup.

"I can help," Kia said. "I'll get a diaper and warm it by the fire!" she called back as she headed to the always full clothesline of clean diapers that dried behind the stove and hung along the partition wall between the kitchen and the storeroom.

Annika removed the heaviest gown from Tomas's dresser drawer. She decided to put two undershirts beneath it. She wouldn't allow Tomas to catch his death of cold.

"You are a wonderful helper," Annika told Kia when she returned with a dry, warmed diaper.

Kia watched as Annika adeptly managed the diaper change and dressed Tomas. "I can wash the diaper," Kia said.

"I'm sure you can. But I had another job in mind," Annika said, and Kia's eyes widened. "I really need someone to rock Tomas while your mor and I do dishes. Are you interested?"

"Yes, I'm big enough."

"I know you are. Let us get the two of you settled."

Kia raced ahead of Annika and climbed into the seat of the rocking chair. Annika trailed behind with Tomas, his Christmas quilt, and a pillow. She tucked the pillow into the chair between Kia and the armrest and settled Tomas in Kia's lap.

"Hold tight while I get another pillow." Annika promptly returned and tucked the second pillow on the opposite side. She covered both with the quilt and instructed Kia. "Please rock Tomas until he goes back to sleep. Don't try to get out of the chair on your own. He's heavier than you think. Call for me, and I'll help you lay him down." She dropped a kiss on Kia's forehead and gave the chair a gentle nudge, and Kia's face glowed.

Annika carried the diaper to the soaking pail in the storeroom. She was worried about Kjerstin, who hadn't moved. Annika poured each a second cup of coffee, sat down across from her, and asked, "What is wrong?"

"I need it to be spring. I couldn't endure this solitude without your company. The thought of you leaving frightens me."

"I won't go far," Annika said. "You are my family. Besides, I depend upon your advice." Annika allowed her eyes to twinkle above the rim of her cup as she sipped.

"What are you talking about?" Kjerstin asked with a precarious arch to her eyebrow.

"Just what I said: you give good advice," Annika said. After a long silence, she continued. "I've decided not to count Oscar out." Annika's cheeks flushed pink, and Kjerstin's tight lips widened to a grin.

◆

Annika couldn't recall exactly when the temperature began to rise and the snowflakes became a lazy drizzle, but she was happy about it. The sun grew warmer and lasted longer each day. Noak walked with a jaunt in his step, and Kjerstin occupied herself with planning for garden planting. Even the children had left for school that morning without complaint, which made the second cup of coffee she shared with Kjerstin and Noak even sweeter. Oscar was continually in Annika's thoughts. If only she knew when to expect him.

She watched Noak and Kjerstin, who had been huddled together over the seed catalog ever since the children left for school. It annoyed Annika. What did they find so intriguing?

"Ahem," Annika said, clearing her throat to gain their attention. Then she asked, "Noak, when do you expect Oscar to return?"

"He'll come home when the work is done. That depends upon the weather and a host of other things. That's the best answer I can give," Noak said, returning to his task.

The answer exasperated Annika. She had no idea what it meant, but she didn't question him further. She rose from the table, gathered the morning dishes, and set about her daily routine. She emptied the water bucket into the stove reservoir and went to the well. She plunked the filled water pail onto the washstand and again interrupted the couple's spring planning.

"Kjerstin, I need something to keep me busy. Would you mind keeping an eye on Tomas while he naps? I thought I'd clean the entry to the root cellar."

"You're making me feel lazy," Kjerstin said with a nod and a chuckle.

Annika snatched the old handmade broom from the porch and disappeared around the corner of the cabin. A rank odor of rotting onions and turnips greeted her when she threw open the entry door to the cellar. She hoped the cellar was less ripe.

The odor transported her back to the New York cellar she and Addie had cleaned only one short year ago. It seemed like forever. Annika stumbled backward, relieved she was in a different world. She gasped for air.

She would meet the foul situation with the same determination that had brought her to it. Annika stepped inside, cut the remaining onions from the rafters, and collected them into a pile near other spoiled odds and ends of cabbage, turnips, and potatoes that had been carried from the cellar but not taken away. Clearing the nasty mess would be easier with a shovel, she realized. While she was at the storage shed, she would bring the hoes and rake back to the root cellar entry, where they were kept during the growing season.

Annika yanked twice on the latch before the storage shed door broke loose. The door swung against the wall, and she stepped into darkness. She felt her way around the shed until her eyes adjusted to the dim light. She inched toward the front corner of the shed where she last had seen the garden tools. A faint outline of a large open barrel informed her that access to the tools was blocked. She grasped the top edge of the barrel and managed to scoot it aside enough to reach the garden tools. She placed them near the doorway and searched for the small shovel she and Kjerstin used to scoop grain. She discovered it hanging from a wall peg that remained just beyond her reach despite her best effort. The scant light from the doorway diminished, but Annika, intent on her task, dismissed it without a thought. She turned away to search for something to step up on—and brushed against someone.

She found herself peering into Oscar's face. Annika's breath stopped, and her heart sang. Oscar's expression twitched into a grin, revealing white teeth beneath his neatly trimmed mustache. He was no longer a shaggy-haired lumberjack; he was her dear Oscar.

"Oscar," she whispered.

They embraced, and she nestled her cheek against his chest. His heart thumped beneath her ear and awoke intense longing. She pulled back and gazed intently into his eyes, unable to decide if she would cry for joy, laugh, or dance.

"Would this be my better time and place?" Oscar asked as he drew her toward him.

Annika nodded consent. His lips caressed hers and stirred emotions that caught Annika unaware. Time stopped.

Oscar relaxed his embrace and pulled away before she was ready. She tightened her embrace and nestled herself against his chest. She savored the moment and realized from that day forward, she would count on Oscar Carlsson.

Oscar lifted her chin and kissed her again before they joined hands and started back to the cabin, leaving the darkness behind.

Printed in the United States
by Baker & Taylor Publisher Services